The Charquery Key

Anita Dewhurst

PREFACE

Tom's eyes suddenly burst open. Blinking to clear the blur from his vision, he felt a throbbing pain pulsing in his head. As a strong scent of woodland wafted into his nose, he gazed around. He was lying on the ground beneath an enormous forest tree.

Clambering to his feet, he ran his fingers through the long strands of black hair tumbling across his forehead. Then he slid them over the contours of his face, each finger trembling as it moved across his nose, mouth, cheeks and chin. He stared down at his body, his breath stuttering out in short, sharp gasps as he tried to make sense of what he saw.

A few moments ago, he had been sitting on a hillside shivering with cold, his weary, bones stiff and aching, his eyes gazing out across a snow-covered winter valley. Now he was standing under an enormous tree at the edge of a wide forest clearing, the colour of the grass so vivid it looked unreal, the sky bluer than anything he had ever seen. What had happened? What had brought him here? And even more weird, what had changed him from a sixty-five-year-old man into a thirteen-year-old boy?

As he peered down a wide path cutting through the trees at the other side of the clearing, a shudder crept down his spine. Someone was watching him - he could feel it. With his ears primed for the slightest crack of a twig or the merest hint of rustling grass he swung around, his eyes darting from side to side, searching the shadowy spaces between the trees. But he saw no one.

This is crazy, he thought. Where am I? He gazed at the gigantic, sprawling tree towering above him, his eyes growing wide when they settled on an enormous golden plaque embedded in the trunk. Glancing cautiously from side to side, he edged closer. The plaque was divided into four equal sections, each named after one of the seasons of the year. At its centre stood a keyhole surrounded by a large, circular loop, to which was attached a gleaming silver arrow. The arrow pointed to the section of the plaque depicting winter.

'Where am I?' Tom cried as a shudder of desperation coursed through him. 'How did I get here?' Clasping his head in his hands he stared at the weird tree, trying to make sense of what was happening. At that moment, an enormous merchant ship floated across his vision, blocking out the trees, blocking out the forest. 'I know that vessel,' he shrieked, watching the dazzling red ensign flapping in the wind. 'It's the Langred Falcon'.

CHAPTER 1

Tom Goodwin was standing on deck as the massive cargo ship eased into Liverpool harbour, its great metal carcass bobbing and swaying like a gigantic hump back whale. The temperature was way below normal for the time of year and as the anchor was weighed he gazed at the mounds of frozen snow heaped around the quayside. He was eager to disembark, make his way to his lodgings and enjoy a fortnight's rest before the start of his next voyage. But as he gazed across the landscape, dotted with ancient church spires and gushing factory chimneys, the scene before him suddenly changed. As if moving through a time warp, it rapidly transformed into an image of Tambley Croft, the tiny village he had run away from over fifty years ago. Weirder still, Tom was instantly overwhelmed by a desperate need to return - to go back to the place he had vowed never to set foot in again.

'Stupid,' he muttered, blinking the vision away. 'Why would I want to go back there?' Slinging his rucksack over his shoulder he pushed through a huddle of rowdy sailors blocking the gangway then made his way down to the dock. But when his feet touched dry land his head begin to swim. It was like standing at the top of an extremely high mountain looking over the edge. Steadying himself on the side rail he took a long, deep breath.

'You all right Tom?' a young deckhand called from behind.

Swinging around, he forced a smile. 'Aye lad. Bit wobbly that's all.'

1

He waited for the deckhand to pass then shuffled along the quayside, where the pungent aroma of oil and hot tar made his queasy stomach churn. Hitching his collar around his face he turned towards one of the narrow alleys leading from the harbour, all he wanted was to get to his lodgings and out of the biting cold as fast as he could.

He hadn't gone far when he jerked to a stop. Swinging around he stared into the noisy crowd gathered on the wharf. There were sailors chatting, merchants discussing trade and dockers unloading cargo, but the voice Tom Goodwin heard calling his name was definitely not one of theirs. It was the strange, echoing voice of a woman. But there were no women in sight. Squeezing his eyes, he scanned the dock again. "Damn!" he growled, banging the side of his head as if trying to realign his ears. 'This is crazy. I need to get some rest.'

Twenty minutes later, Tom arrived at the Sailors Home in Canning Place, and as he entered the enormous hall, the pungent smell of bleach and carbolic soap invaded his nose. He was greeted by the chief housekeeper, an elderly woman who, because of his many visits, knew him well.

After dealing with the formalities, Tom arrived at his first floor room, threw his holdall on the bare wooden boards, draped his damp coat across the back of a chair then lay on the bed to get some rest. Whatever was ailing him would be gone after a good nap. But just as he started to drift into sleep he felt a presence, it was as though someone else was in the room with him.

He leapt off the bed, his eyes darting from the window to the door and back again, his body stiff and wary. Striding to the wardrobe he wrenched it open. It was empty. Turning, he glanced around the room then got down on his hands and

2

knees and stared into the dark, empty space beneath the bed. All he could see was a thin layer of dust. Clambering to his feet, trying to figure out what was going on, he suddenly bolted upright. Standing absolutely still he gazed anxiously around the room, his breath held tight in the back of his throat. The same echoing voice he had heard on the quayside was whispering his name, 'Tom . . . Tom . . . '

Hurrying to the door he yanked it open. There was no one in the corridor outside. He darted to the window, brushed a cobweb from the glass and peered out. The street below was empty. 'Must be going mad,' he mumbled. 'I need to get some sleep.'

Shuffling back to the bed he eased himself down and letting out a sigh of exasperation, gazed in bewilderment at the ceiling. But just as his eyes were about to close, he spotted something lodged between the layers of flaky paintwork. As soon as his gaze locked onto it, it started to grow, swaying slowly from side to side as it spread across the empty space. Within seconds he was staring again at an image of Tambley Croft, just as it had looked when he was a boy. He recognised the tumbling waters of the river, the tiny cottage by the mill, details so clear he could almost reach out and touch them.

'Tom,' he heard the echoing voice whisper. 'You must go back.'

Leaping from the bed he grabbed his coat from the back of the chair and hurried out of the door.

It was dark when Tom arrived back at his lodgings, but even though it was late, he insisted on being given a different room, a request that made him far from popular with the resident matron. Every night for the following week, his dreams took him back to Tambley Croft and each morning when he woke up, he felt a desperate need to go back. He tried hard to push the feeling away, to force it from his mind. But it was no use. As each day went by the overpowering longing to return to the place of his childhood grew stronger and stronger. Finally, three days before he was due to set sail he checked out of the Sailors Home, cancelled his forthcoming voyage and set off on the long journey home.

Battered by icy winds, hampered by tracts of frozen snow, he arrived in Tambley just before dawn on the twenty-first day of March. He didn't know why he was there. All he knew as he settled on Molly's Crag, a rocky outcrop on the outskirts of the village, was that it felt right. And at long last, the relentless churning in his stomach and battering of his brain had ceased.

Clinging to the damp coat hugging his shivering body he stared into the snow covered valley, where swirls of smoke billowing from tiny cottages chimneys, darkened an already miserable sky. Eventually his eyes came to rest on an ancient windmill hugging the banks of the river - its huge wooden wheel rotted and still, its broken sails dangling like severed arms. Shifting his gaze to a small stone cottage standing in its shadow, the tiny bedroom window shielded from view by the branches of an enormous Sycamore, a pang of nostalgia shuddered through him. He remembered being happy there, that was until the day his father was killed in an accident at the mill. Years later, after his mother remarried then died in a riding accident, he used to hide in the tree to escape the drunken rages of his hideous step-father.

As he moved his gaze along the icy waters of the river, stopping at a place where it swept around a wide, hairpin bend, Tom felt a chill shudder through him. The surge of water was so turbulent that even the ice could not restrain it,

4

and as he glared at the raging torrent, he remembered the fateful day that was to change his life forever.

Tom was thirteen years old when Badger - the little dog his father had given him just before he died - accidentally fell into the river. It happened at the widest point of the bend where raging currents crossed and swirled. Badger instantly disappeared but Tom dived in after him, and though it took a while to battle his way through the swirling flurry, when he reached the bottom he managed to grab Badger by the scruff of his neck and haul him out. The little dog was alive, but his breathing was shallow and his eyes dull and glazed. Tom wrapped him in his jumper and raced for home.

When he entered the cottage, his drunken step-father, his eyes wild and angry, staggered towards him wielding a thick, leather belt. Desperate to get out of his way, Tom dashed up the stairs. But when he reached the third step from the top he tripped and slid all the way down, banging his head on the bare wooden treads as he went. Still clinging to Badger he rose shakily to his feet, and luckily, saw his step-father slumped in a heap on the floor. Tom hurried to his room, eased his aching body down on the bed then carefully unfolded the soaking jumper from around his little dog. But it was too late - Badger was dead.

Tom spent most of the night crying. When dawn broke, he wrapped Badger in a soft woollen blanket, crammed a few clothes into an old leather bag and crept silently from the cottage. He made his way to Molly's Crag, buried Badger close to an old, solitary tree then ran across the fields towards Bradshaw's farm. There, he could cut through the stable yard onto a single track road leading away from the village. He knew he risked being seen, but he had to tell his friend Maggie Bradshaw why he was leaving.

When he reached the farmyard it looked deserted. He crept past the barn, eased his way around the hen house and headed towards the stables. For the past few days Maggie had been spending most of her time with a new born foal. He prayed she would be there now.

'Tom!' she gasped, when he poked his head around the stable door, 'I was just . . .' But when she saw the bruises on his face, her smile suddenly faded. 'Tom! What happened?'

'Badger's dead,' he said, squeezing his eyes to hold back the tears. 'I buried him up on Molly's Crag. The fat pig was drunk again last night, came at me with his belt, ready to crack me one. I would've saved Badger but for him. I hate him!'

"Oh, Tom!"

"I'm going to Liverpool, see if I can find work on a ship. If I tell 'em I'm fifteen, they'll probably take me on, take me as far away from here as I can get. Promise you won't tell. I don't want anyone coming after me. Don't want them bringing me back. I never want to see this place again. Ever!"

"I promise," Maggie said, squeezing his hand. "I'll never tell a soul. But I wish you weren't going Tom. I'll miss you so much."

"I'll miss you too," he whispered.

"Here," she said, pulling a shiny coin from her pocket. "This penny's brand new. It'll bring you luck."

Tom sighed as he turned it over in his fingers. "You know what! Some day I'm going to do something special . . .

something amazing . . . and when I do I'll get this penny back to you - just so as you'll know."

Suddenly stirred from his thoughts, Tom felt something brush the side of his face. "Who's there?" he cried, clambering to his feet. "Who's there?"

He was standing close to the spot where he had buried Badger all those years ago. Behind him a winter ravaged tree creaked and groaned in the freezing northerly wind, but he could hear something else - something he recognised - a woman's voice whispering his name.

Swinging around, he saw the tree trunk shimmering like sunlight on water. Beside it stood a young woman with long silver hair and a billowing green cloak. He had never seen anyone as beautiful in all his life. "What! . . . Who! . . . Where did you come from?"

"I am Norva," she smiled, her blue eyes sparkling like sapphires. "I am the spirit of springtime."

"The spirit of springtime!" Tom moved a step closer, his wary eyes squeezing to slits. "Don't be ridiculous!"

"I need your help Tom."

"Needing help is one matter. Pretending to be some kind of nature spirit to get it is another. And anyway . . . how do you know my name?"

Without answering she moved to the centre of the crag and raising her hand, made a circular movement over the ground. At that very instant the thick ice melted away and a carpet of lush green grass surrounded by a hundreds of bright yellow daffodils sprang from the rock.

"Today is the first day of spring - the Vernal Equinox. Before noon tomorrow the Vertrius Gate must be opened. If it is not, your world will be doomed to eternal winter.' Turning to Tom she held out her hand. "That is why I called you. We desperately need your help."

"You . . . You made me come back?"

"Yes,' she said, smiling. "Come, join me in the circle and I will explain."

"You can't be real!" Tom gasped, edging closer. "This is crazy . . . " Stepping over the daffodils he sat down on the grass. ". . . or . . . I'm going mad."

"I had to call you," Norva said, sitting beside him. "We desperately need your help."

"We? Who's we?"

"Those responsible for keeping your world in order, ensuring each season comes and goes exactly as it should."

"You mean . . . nature spirits . . . you're not joking?"

"No Tom. I'm not joking."

'Nature spirits!' Tom exclaimed again.

"Let me explain. Then maybe you will understand."

"I don't see how I can understand something that doesn't exist," Tom mumbled, his forehead creased into a frown.

Gazing across the frozen landscape, Norva smiled. "Nature spirits come from Keeros, a parallel universe existing in another dimension. Keeros is governed by a council of wizards known as Keepers. Their task is to ensure the

8

seasons of earth come and go exactly as they should, summer, autumn, winter and spring - it has always been so . . . until now."

"Until now?" Tom asked. "What do you mean?"

"Arcos, the spirit of winter, refuses to relinquish his allotted winter span. Aided by sinister forces from the Blacklands, he has stolen the Charquery Key - the only means by which the Vertrius gate can be unlocked, and should we fail to retrieve it before the equinox ends, the power of the Keepers will be destroyed and your world plunged into perpetual winter. Tropical lands will freeze, millions will perish and as time goes by, the entire human race will become extinct. We must stop him now, before it is too late. That is why I called you."

"Me . . . but . . . "

'The only power capable of defeating Arcos is Zafror, the mighty element of fire. He dwells within a vast fortress of rock deep within the Mountain of Delnar. We need a messenger - someone unknown on Keeros - someone who can slip through Arcos's evil web to seek Zafror's help.'

"What? You want me to be the messenger?"

"Yes," Norva said, rising to her feet. "You are our only hope."

"That's ridiculous! I'm an old man! What can I do?"

"Tom' she said, smiling softly. "I am the spirit of springtime - the essence of renewal. I bring youth where there is age, hope where there is despair. I can make you young again."

"Young again!"

"All you need do is place your hand in mine. Together we will journey to another world. Another dimension. Please Tom . . . Take my hand."

Rising to his feet he gazed into her radiant blue eyes. "This has got to be a dream," he said. Shaking his head from side to side he smiled pensively, then, with a shudder of unease, placed his old, wrinkled hand into hers. "I'm going to wake up in a minute."

CHAPTER 2

Tom stood there staring at his hands and feet, realising now what had changed him from an old man into a thirteen-year-old boy.

Tilting his head back, he stared into the gigantic tree towering above him, it was twice as tall and three times as wide as any of the others. Gasping with disbelief he moved his gaze slowly down the trunk until his eyes came to rest on a gleaming golden shield embedded in the wood. The shield was divided into four equal quarters, each section representing a season of the year. At its centre sat a keyhole encircled by a large silver ring. Attached to the ring, an arrow pointed the section representing winter.

'This is the Everlasting Tree,' Norva whispered.

Spinning around, Tom squealed with delight. 'Norva,' he cried, 'I'm young again, just like you said. I can't believe it!' Smiling, she watched him gaze around the forest, an expression of total amazement on his face. 'Is this Keeros?' he said at last. 'It looks just like earth.'

'Yes. This is Keeros, and though it is similar to earth in many ways, it is also very different.

'Different how?' Tom asked.

Keeros is divided into two separate halves by an invisible barrier through which no one can pass. This side of Keeros always faces the sun, which never, ever sets, and as it is always day time, there is no need of sleep. The other side, known as the Blacklands, lies in semi-darkness.

'Wow!' Tom exclaimed, quickly digesting the information before moving on to the next question. 'Why is that tree so huge? And what's that?' He was pointing to the golden shield.

'This is the Everlasting Tree, where everything begins and everything ends. The mechanism in its trunk regulates the seasons of your earth. At the beginning of each new season, the Charquery Key is used to open the Vertrius Gate, which sets the change of season into motion. As you can see, the key is missing.'

'And you want me to get it back,' Tom said.

'You are our only hope. Soon your journey to retrieve the Charquery Key will begin, but first we must visit the eastern wizard, he has prepared a map to guide you. Come, we must hurry.'

They moved quickly through the forest, navigating a tangle of dusty trails that twisted and turned like lifeless serpents. Eventually they came to a barrier of giant ferns that stood so tall and were packed so tight, it was impossible to see a way through.

'What do we do now?' Tom asked.

Norva smiled as she moved forward and when she drew close to the leafy barrier, a section of foliage bent to the ground, creating a narrow passageway. 'Follow me,' she called.

As they hurried along the path, the ferns swished back into place behind them and soon they emerged into a tranquil glade fringed with ornamental grasses and wild flowers. A peculiar looking tree, resembling an immense leaf covered dome, stood at the very centre of the glade, its mass of

12

luxuriant branches cascading like the waters of a fountain to the ground, where they appeared to be embedded in the earth.

'This is the Abalon tree,' Norva said as they drew close. 'Where Altair Devole, the eastern wizard lives.'

'He lives inside a tree?' Tom grinned. 'How do we get in?'

When she placed her hand on one of the leafy spirals there was a loud rustle of leaves followed by the groan of creaking wood, then an opening appeared just large enough for them to pass through.

Expecting a dark, gloomy interior, Tom gasped when they entered a bright, sunny garden, much bigger and more spacious than anything he could have imagined from the outside. Cascades of delicately perfumed blossom festooned the inner walls, a cushion of soft, green grass covered the ground beneath his feet and a blaze of brilliant sunlight flooded from above. 'Amazing!' he muttered, trying to figure out how it could be possible.

At the centre of the garden stood a gnarled tree trunk, its bark so thick and knobbly, its shape so distorted, it looked like some kind of prehistoric monster. A small door at the base of the trunk gaped open. Above it sat a wooden plaque inscribed with a rhyme:

> *'Welcome seasons come and go*
> *Summer, autumn winter snow*
> *Springtime promise here beheld*
> *All in tune with nature's weld'*

As Tom followed Norva through the door a shudder of nerves jangled his stomach when he found himself staring down a narrow, spiral stairway. 'Looks a bit spooky,' he

13

whispered as he watched it twist into darkness around the trunk of the tree.

Reaching inside her cloak Norva produced a small, glass orb which radiated a dim halo of light. 'Stay close,' she said.

They descended the stairs slowly, the glow from the orb barely enough to keep their faces visible and the space so cramped it was difficult for Tom to know where to place his feet. When they rounded the final bend, they came into a narrow passageway where a shaft of light from a half open door illuminated the darkness. From somewhere inside the room, the soft breathing notes of a flute drifted through the silence.

Returning the orb to her cloak, Norva tapped on the door. At that very moment the music stopped, then a loud clatter followed by the sound of approaching footsteps could be heard.

When the door swung open, a chubby little man with dancing blue eyes and a mischievous smile appeared. 'At last,' he grinned, peering over the top of his wire rimmed spectacles. 'Come in my friends. Come in.'

As Tom followed Norva into the large, oddly shaped room, his attention was immediately drawn to movement, coming from somewhere above his head. Looking up he saw a tangled mass of tree roots with what appeared to be a miniature universe suspended in the air below them. Several small planets were rotating around a fiery red sun.

'I've never seen anything like that before!' he gasped. 'What is it?'

The chubby little man chuckled as he closed the door behind them. 'It's a Phelseon Map, an intricate and rather complex miniature of your solar system.'

'But what's that?' Tom said, pointing to a small, semi-translucent planet covered in silver mist. It was smaller than the moon in size but was tracking the earth in exactly the same orbit.

'That is Keeros,' the wizard grinned. 'Invisible to your world because it exists in a different dimension.'

'Wow!' Tom whispered. 'That's amazing.'

As he gazed around the room, calmed by the tranquil, moonlike glow radiating from the walls, he saw row after row of shelves filled with bottles, potions, maps and telescopes. The floor was similarly littered with books, metronomes and strange looking clocks ticking away in harmony. At the very centre of the jumble sat an old, comfy looking armchair.

'I'm quite good at some things,' the strange little man said, when he saw the look of bewilderment on Tom's face, 'but tidiness is not one of them.' His eyes glowed with warmth as he swept a low bow. 'I am Altair Devole, otherwise known as the eastern wizard. And you must be Tom.'

Before Tom had a chance to respond, the wizard hurried towards one of the bulging shelves, returning moments later with a scroll of yellow parchment. 'I expect Norva has told you of our dilemma?' he smiled.

'Yes' Tom said, staring curiously at an old shoe hanging from the wizard's tunic.

'She has explained how Arcos has stolen the Charquery key and how we need you to get it back before equinox passes?'

'Yes,' Tom said, his eyes still glued to the shoe.

'And you are not afraid?'

'I .. Er .. No! .. I mean .. I've not really thought about it!'

'I see,' the wizard nodded. 'Well in that case, we must get you on your way. Every moment spent here is a moment lost.' He slid the parchment from under his arm and spread it carefully across a small wooden table.

'For safety reasons this map has been divided in two separate halves. This portion details your journey through Bragenon Forest then out across the Plain of Zantor, where you will enter the Kingdom of the Festinol. The Festinol King awaits your arrival and will provide you with the second half of the map, which contains directions for the final part of journey to the Mountain of Delnar. He will also advise you of how to make contact with Zafror, the mighty element of fire.'

The wizard's chubby finger traced a thin, red line across the parchment. 'This is the Trail of Medioc and is the only path you must follow. It runs from the Everlasting tree here - where your journey both begins and ends - all the way to the Mountain of Delnar.' He pointed to a vast mountain close to the edge of the parchment. 'When you leave the safety of our forest you must cross the River of Separation, at the bottom of the river sleeps a mighty serpent. His name is Pyrus Thangor and he is capable of swallowing boys like you whole. You must take great care, for when his sleep is disturbed, he is ill tempered and hostile. Cross swiftly by the wooden bridge here,' he indicated a narrow structure spanning the water, 'and you will be safe.'

16

Sliding his finger to a vast area of woodland on the other side of the river he said, 'This is Bragenon Forest, the only route you can take to reach the mountain. Arcos's fortress, which stands at the very centre of this forest, surrounds the Pit of Pendurak - a dark, malevolent abyss which, until recently, has been inaccessible. When Arcos set out on his journey of treachery, he enlisted the help of dark forces from the Blacklands. Together they succeeded in opening the pit. The evil it unleashes not only imbues him with great power, it sends forth malevolent creatures to help guard the Charquery Key. '

'You must travel quickly and quietly so as not to alert Arcos to your presence, but whatever happens, you must stay on the Trail of Medioc. Do not stray from its path. Should you meet anyone along the way, it is vital that you keep your destination a secret. If anyone asks, say you are visiting the Festinol and leave it at that.'

Pulling a small, white mask from his pocket, the wizard handed it to Tom.

'Keep this with you at all times. It will protect you from the Skrorth - vile creatures Arcos has summoned from the pit. Their task is to protect the forest from anyone wanting to challenge him. They immobilise their victims with poisonous gas then suffocate them slowly with stinking slime. They are easily recognised by the long, hooded robes that conceal their hideous forms and their odour can be detected long before they are seen. Should you get the whiff of a repulsive stench, tie this mask around your face and stay out of sight until it is safe to continue.

'When you reach the other side of Bragenon, you will emerge from the forest at the edge of the Plain of Zantor. Continue along the trail until it splits into two, then take the right track until you come to a large, flat topped boulder - the entrance to the Festinol Kingdom.'

The wizard untied the shoe hanging from his belt and handed it to Tom. 'The boulder has a footprint carved into the top. To gain entry to the kingdom you must place this shoe directly into the mould.'

'Will the Festinol know who I am?' Tom asked, tying the shoe to his belt.

'Indeed they will. They await your arrival. When you are in possession of the second part of the map you must continue along the trail to the Mountain of Delnar. Once inside, Zafror will give you the means of retrieving the Charquery Key. To reclaim it, you must return to Bragenon forest and enter Arcos's fortress.' Pausing, the wizard leaned close to Tom's ear and lowering his voice whispered, 'There may be times you will be so afraid you will not want to go on. But you must. Once your journey begins, there is no turning back. Therefore, if you feel unable to undertake this dangerous task, if you wish to return to your own world with no recollection of our meeting or the events to come - you must tell me now.' He stared deep into Tom's eyes. 'You must be certain. There is no other way.'

Tom stuffed the mask into his pocket, his shoulders rising and falling with the depth of the breaths he was taking. 'I am certain,' he said. 'I want to get the key.'

'Very well. The time has come for your journey to begin. Norva will escort you to the edge of the forest. From there you are on your own. Once the key is in your possession you must return to the Everlasting Tree as fast as you can. Only then will our worlds be safe.'

18

After Tom had tucked the map down the front of his shirt, the wizard led him and Norva to the top of the spiral stairway.

'Remember,' he said, as they entered the sunny garden. 'Stay on the Trail of Medioc, tell no one of your destination and most of all, watch for a yellowing sky.

'A yellowing sky?' Tom frowned. 'What does that mean?'

'It signals the end of equinox. When the time draws near the sky will turn yellow and should the Vertrius Gate remain locked, black clouds of night will roll in from the east. Then, when darkness closes above, when not a single vestige of light remains, Keeros will be destroyed and the earth left to the mercy of Arcos and the evil forces that control him.'

'Oh!' Tom exclaimed, half wishing he had never asked.

As he watched Norva lead Tom towards the secret doorway, Altair Devole sighed heavily, shook his head slowly from side to side then turned back to the tree. But just as he was about to make his way down the stairway, he suddenly swung around and rushed back into the garden. 'Wait!' he called, 'I nearly forgot! Stop! Don't go any further!'

As Tom and Norva swung around, they saw the wizard scurrying behind the tree trunk looking extremely flustered. 'Close your eyes Tom,' he shouted. 'Keep them closed until I tell you to look!'

Puzzled, Tom turned to Norva. 'What . . . ?'

'Are they closed?' the wizard cried urgently. 'Are they tight?

'Yes!' Tom said, squeezing his eyes together. 'But . . . '

19

There was a rustle of leaves followed by the hurried patter of approaching footsteps.

'Very well, 'the wizard said breathlessly. 'Now you can look.'

When Tom's eyes burst open, Altair Devole and Norva were standing side by side. The wizard looked remarkably pleased about something and Norva was grinning broadly. Tom looked slowly from one to the other, trying to figure out what was going on.

'What?' he asked, looking puzzled, 'what is it?'

Without a word Devole and Norva drew apart and as the space between them widened, Tom saw a small, black dog sitting on the grass, its head turned towards a pool of running water.

His heart skipped a beat . . It couldn't be . . .

'Badger?'

The dog's head shot around, its ears pricked up, its nose twitched and sniffed. Then, with a sudden yelp of recognition it leapt straight into Tom's outstretched arms.

'Badger!' he yelled as tears flooded his eyes. 'I don't believe it!'

'He's waited a long time for this,' the wizard chuckled.

'But how?' Tom spluttered, clutching the wriggling animal to his chest.

'He is here. That's all that matters.'

'Can he go with me?' Tom gasped.

'Of course,' the wizard said. 'He will be with you as long as you remain on Keeros.'

.

CHAPTER 3

Tom and Badger followed Norva back to the Everlasting Tree. From there they crossed the sunny clearing and continued along a wide path edged with tall trees and bracken. They eventually emerged from the forest at the top of a shallow incline, stopping at the edge of a flower fringed track that wound its way down to a slow, meandering river.

The water looked calm and inviting, stretching into the distance as far as the eye could see, and a little way to the right its smooth, glassy surface reflected the image of an old wooden bridge. Shading his eyes from the glare, Tom glanced along the ancient structure until his gaze settled on a stretch of black, leafless woodland hugging the top of the opposite bank.

'The Forest of Bragenon,' Norva whispered. 'Once a beautiful place. Now it is dying, chilled by the evil taking refuge in its heart.'

A shudder quivered Tom's spine as he stared at the decimated forest. 'Is that where Arcos's fortress is?'

Norva lowered her eyes and nodded, then, pointing to the dusty track running down to the water's edge she said, 'This is the Trail of Medioc. The only path you must follow. It will take you through Bragenon Forest, across the Plain of Zantor, then all the way to the mountain of Delnar.' Turning to Tom she squeezed his hand. 'I have to go,' she said. 'We must not be seen together. Travel quickly and quietly and whatever happens, stick to the Trail of Medioc.'

For a moment Tom sensed fear within her, but the moment was shattered when Badger started leaping up and down barking at the sky. Swinging around Tom saw the biggest bird he had ever seen circling the bridge, its wingspan almost as wide as the bridge was long.

'What's that?' he gasped, 'It's huge!'

'It's a Skrell' Norva whispered.

Tom stood motionless, his eyes bulging wide. 'Where did it come from?' But his question was met with silence. Turning full circle, he looked around, his heart beating rapidly. 'Norva!' he whispered, staring along the dusty track. But Norva had vanished.

Swinging back to the river, he watched the Skrell gliding from one end of the bridge to the other, its head moving slowly from side to side, its predatory eyes searching the wooden structure. Suddenly realising Badger would make a tasty meal for the bird, Tom swooped down low to lift him from the ground, but in his haste he stepped on the little dog's paw and when a frantic yelp rang out across the valley, the bird's enormous head shot around.

'Quick!' Tom yelled, running for the safety of a nearby bush. 'It's seen us.' He yanked Badger under a tangle of knotted branches then lay on top of him. 'Don't make a sound,' he whispered.

Moments later he heard an ominous thud.

Peering out from under the bush he saw the bird's massive talons crashing along the ground towards him. Moments later it let out an ear piercing screech and started tearing at the branches, sending leaves and twigs scattering in all directions. Fearful that the creature would break through, Tom shielded Badger against the dusty earth then quickly searched the ground for something sharp. When his fingers

23

touched the end of a thick, broken stick, he stretched his arm as far as he could and dragged it towards him. But just as he was about to jab it at the bird, the bush fell still.

Tom remained motionless, his heart pounding in his chest, beads of sweat trickling down the sides of his face. What was happening? Hardly daring to breathe he listened hard, trying to figure out what the bird was doing, then all of a sudden he heard the beat of powerful wings. Pulling himself to his knees he peered through a knot of broken twigs and saw the massive predator rising into the sky. He could hardly believe his luck. When the creature finally disappeared from view he lifted Badger into his arms then crawled into the open. 'Come on,' he whispered, 'let's go before it comes back.'

They hurried down to the river then turned in the direction of the bridge. Remembering the wizard's warning about the serpent, Pyrus Thangor, Tom kept his eyes constantly on the water, while Badger, still shaken by the thought of being eaten alive, kept his eyes fixed firmly on the sky.

When they approached the bridge, Tom got a whiff of a nauseating stench - like decaying cabbage and rotten eggs all rolled into one. 'Ugh!'

Pinching his nose, he crept forward until he was standing at the very edge of the crossing. It was then he saw the thick globules of green slime hanging from the bridge rails and covering the planks. 'Yuk,' he gasped, his stomach churning. 'How are we going to cross that?'

Tilting his head as far back as he could, he quickly scanned the sky. 'Come on Badger. We've got to try. We must get across before the Skrell comes back.'

He stepped hesitantly onto the slippery planks and when he grabbed hold of the bridge rail, the thick, gooey substance oozed through his fingers. With a look of absolute disgust, he slithered awkwardly along, while Badger, closer to the ground and more stable on four legs, appeared to be negotiating the obstacle with ease.

They gradually edged their way to the centre of the bridge, where, pausing to catch his breath, Tom leaned over the side to look at the river. He could see the image of his head and shoulders reflected in the water. Then something else caught his attention. Moving his gaze to the right, he saw a cluster of large bubbles. He stared at them curiously, wondering what they could be. Then all of a sudden, his heart skipped a beat. Two enormous orange eyes were staring at him from just beneath the surface, making him swing around so hard he almost slid over the edge.

'Come on Badger. Let's get out of here.'

They navigated the second half of the bridge much faster than the first and were soon standing on the opposite bank, a steep, grassy slope interlaced with several dusty trails. Tom was sure the Trail of Medioc was the one leading directly from the bridge, but to be absolutely certain, he decided to consult the map. When he plunged his hand into his jacket pocket his face suddenly screwed to a frown - the parchment wasn't there. He quickly searched through the rest of his pockets then, feeling a twinge of panic, he ripped off his jacket and turned it inside out. 'The map's gone,' he cried.

Pacing up and down he tried to figure out where it could be, and as he thought about the Skrell's attack, and how he had shuffled around under the bush, he turned and gazed across the river. It must be over there. 'I've got to go back,' he said, reaching down to stroke Badger's head. 'Stay here. Don't try to follow me.'

He ran down the slope then slithered back along the slippery bridge planks as fast as he could. When he got to the other side he leapt onto the bank, raced along the water's edge then up the slope until he reached the bush. Scrambling underneath, he saw the map lying beneath a scattering of broken twigs. Puffing out a huge sigh of relief he snatched it up, stuffed it down the side of his sock then sprinted back to the bridge.

He was almost half way across when he saw Badger, his ears flattened to his head, his tail tucked between his legs, sliding along the planks towards him. 'No!' he yelled, 'Go back!'

With this momentary lapse of concentration Tom's hands suddenly slipped from the rail. Unable to keep his balance he crashed to the floor, slid along the slippery planks and went crashing through the bridge rails like a battering ram.

Plunging feet first into the water he descended like a speeding bullet. Terrified the serpent would soon be after him he waited for the momentum too slow, then fighting hard against the drag, forced his way back to the top. Bursting through the surface he gulped a huge lungful of air then quickly scanned the river. The water was clear, Pyrus Thangor was nowhere in sight. But as he turned in the direction of Badger, who was leaping up and down on the bank yelping in frenzy, he saw an enormous black shadow darken the ground.

'No!' he screamed, as the Skrell flew rapidly towards them.

Swimming as fast as he could he sped towards the bank, trying to reach Badger before the massive predator could snatch him away. But as the bird swooped down, moving closer and closer, Tom suddenly realised that Badger was not its prey, it was heading straight for him.

26

He dived beneath the surface, his eyes bulging wide as he twirled in the water searching for the serpent. He saw nothing. Holding his breath, he tried to stay beneath the surface, when all of a sudden he felt a massive tremor coming from somewhere below. Looking down, he saw an enormous black shape surging from the darkness. It was then that something thudded into his back and as two huge talons clamped around his body, he felt himself being hoisted into the air.

The Skrell had him firmly in its grasp but hampered by the weight of its water drenched wings it started drifting back to down to the river. At that moment, Pyrus Thangor's massive head burst through the surface. Sounding an angry roar, he lunged at the retreating bird and as his jaws clashed together, missing Tom by inches, they caught hold of the shoe dangling from his waist. With the Skrell pulling one way and the serpent pulling the other way, the string holding the shoe snapped in two, sending the massive serpent crashing back into the water.

Screeching triumphantly the Skrell climbed higher, but struggling against the heaviness of its waterlogged wings it drifted back towards the bank, where Badger was whirling around screaming in frenzy. As it swept over the little dog's head he sprang from the ground, landed on Tom's back and snarling viciously, sank his needle sharp teeth deep into the creature's leg. With a determined growl, he twisted and tugged until suddenly, a deep wound burst open and blood spurted down his face. With a loud shriek of pain, the bird released its grip and as Tom and Badger thudded to the ground, it soared up into the sky.

Quickly scrambling to his feet Tom lifted Badger into his arms, his heart was thudding fast and his body trembling. Swinging around he glared at the river. Pyrus Thangor's

27

massive head was poking through the surface of the water, his enraged eyes watching the Skrell speeding further and further away.

'Come on,' Tom gasped, putting Badger back on the ground. 'Let's go before it comes back.'

Not daring to stop to examine the map he hurried up the path he thought was the right one.

At the top of the slope stood a towering mass of dark, brooding woodland, where frost damaged leaves fluttered to the ground like clouds of black confetti. A few moments ago, knowing he would be safe from the prying eyes of the Skrell, Tom had been eager to reach the cover of the forest. Now, faced with a cold, hostile environment shrouded in eerie silence, he was not so sure. He edged into the gloomy half light with Badger trotting close to his heels, his eyes darting rapidly from side to side, scanning the shadowy spaces between the trees.

They hurried along the trail as quietly as they could until they came to a sharp bend shrouded with tall, overhanging trees. Slowing to a walk, Tom felt a sudden blast of cold air press against his skin and noticed the sparse patches of grass running along the edge of the trail were now white with frost. Hugging his jacket closer to his body he was about to quicken his pace, when Badger suddenly stopped dead. His ears pricked up, the fur on the back of his neck stood on end and a low growl rumbled deep in his throat. Grabbing him by the collar, Tom yanked him behind a blackened tree.

'Stay quiet,' he whispered, catching a whiff of the same repulsive stench they had encountered at the bridge. Holding his breath, he moved his head slowly around the tree trunk until he could see the path. Then he suddenly dodged back, fear pulsing through him like an electric shock. A black, robed figure was moving along the trail towards them.

When the creature drew level with the tree, a plume of purple smoke slithered from the sleeve if its robe then crept up the bark to the few remaining leaves clinging to the topmost branches. The instant it touched them they withered and fell, then fluttered to the ground like burnt paper. The stench was unbearable. Tom clamped his hand over his mouth, but the air was so thick with fumes, his throat began to burn and his lungs felt as though they were about to explode. As his head flooded with dizziness and his legs turned weak and shaky, he suddenly remembered the mask. Yanking it from his pocket he flattened himself against the tree and clamped it to his face. Breath after breath of sweet, fresh air flooded into his lungs and within moments he was back to normal. Gripping tight onto the tree trunk, he poked his head around and peered out. The Skrorth was moving away, completely unaware of his presence.

Heaving a sigh, he slid back out of sight, pulled the mask from his face and pushed it back into his pocket. Suddenly glimpsing movement in the corner of his eye, he spun around expecting to see Badger, but what he saw sent shock waves surging through his body.

A peculiar looking dwarf, its skin, hair and clothes blue from head to toe, was propped against a tree with Badger sprawled unconscious in its arms. 'Don't be alarmed,' it whispered, its mouth twisting to a lopsided grin, 'I'm here to help.'

Sprinting forward, Tom grabbed the mask and clamping it firmly around Badger's mouth, watched anxiously as he breathed in the clean, fresh air. When the little dog's eyes fluttered open he wagged his tail and started licking Tom's hand, but the instant he noticed the ugly creature leering over

29

him, he leapt to the ground snarling viciously. Afraid Badger's anger may attract the Skrorth's attention Tom lifted him into his arms and gently closed his fingers around his muzzle. 'It's okay,' he said. 'It's okay.'

'I'm sorry I startled you,' the creature said, its huge, bulbous eyes exaggerating the ugliness of its flat, squashed up face. 'I saw your predicament with the Skrorth and tried to warn you.'

'Who are you?' Tom asked, suddenly noticing the sword strapped to the creature's back.

'I am Brignar, one of the blue dwarfs of Bragenon. 'And . . . if you don't mind me asking . . . who are you?'

'Tom. My name's Tom.'

'Well, you must be either crazy or desperate to be travelling through here. You know Bragenon is teeming with Skrorth?' As he spoke his gaze settled on the mask dangling from Tom's fingers. 'Of course you must know. You have come prepared.' He slowly backed away, his eyes still riveted on the mask. 'To be travelling through this forest armed with protection, can mean only one thing. You are on your way to the Mountain of Delnar.'

'Delnar!' Tom exclaimed, quickly shoving the mask into his pocket. 'Don't be ridiculous! I'm on my way to visit the Festinol.'

'No one would risk travelling this road to visit the Festinol. No one would risk travelling this road unless it was a matter of life or death. Arcos knows that sooner or later, someone will try to reach Delnar to seek Zafror's help. He has ordered the Skrorth to lie in ambush further along the trail. You will never get past them.' Moving closer to Tom, the dwarf

30

lowered his voice to a whisper. 'There is another way of getting through Bragenon, a way known only to blue dwarfs. Beneath this forest runs a complex maze of tunnels. One of them runs directly beneath the Trail of Medioc. If you follow me, I will make sure you reach the other side of the forest safely.'

'No!' Tom snapped. 'I will stay on the trail. And anyway,' he said, glaring at the dwarf suspiciously, 'why are you offering me help. You don't even know me!'

'The dwarf's eyes suddenly filled with tears. 'This forest is my home,' he whimpered. 'The only place I have ever lived. Before Arcos unleashed the horrors of Pendurak it was filled with warmth and beauty. Now, because of his evil deeds, it is dying. If you are trying to reach Delnar then I want to help you, I want to make sure you get there safely so that this forest can be purged of evil. If, as you say, you are merely travelling to the Festinol Kingdom, then travelling under ground will keep you out of harm's way. You will never get past the Skrorth if you stay on the surface.'

'I'm sorry,' Tom said, feeling a twinge of pity for the dwarf. 'I am sure your intentions are good, and . . . I don't want to sound mean or anything but . . . how do I know you're telling me the truth? How do I know the Skrorth are waiting in ambush? How do I know I can trust you?'

'My sword,' Brignar cried, sliding the gleaming weapon from its sheath 'is the most powerful weapon in the land. Witness its power! Feel the fear my enemies feel!' With a sudden, dramatic flourish he sliced through a hefty branch hanging from a nearby tree and as it thudded to the ground, he ran back to Tom and rammed the sword into the earth by his feet. 'Take it,' he said. 'In return, give me your trust.'

As a wave of shock coursed through his veins Tom glared at the gleaming weapon. 'You want me to have your sword?'

'I am powerless without it,' Brignar smiled, 'but if it helps you to trust me, then it's yours until we get you safely to the other side of the forest.

'I . . . I don't know what to say.

'Just try it,' Brignar grinned, 'It will surprise you.'

When Tom placed his hand on the sword he felt a rush of energy surge through him. Raising the weapon up he held it in front of his face and as his eyes glared into the gleaming blade, he gasped when he saw that the image reflected in the metal was not his, but that of the blue dwarf.

'The blade reflects only the image of its owner,' Brignar whispered.

Tom was now in a quandary, he didn't know what to do. The wizard had told him to stay on the Trail of Medioc, but how could he if the Skrorth were waiting to ambush him? Turning to Brignar, he said, 'You say there's a tunnel running below Medioc?'

'That's right. It runs directly beneath it all the way through the forest. In a way, it's part of the Trail of Medioc.'

Altair Devole had said nothing about travelling beneath the trail, and it would, in fact, be almost the same as travelling on the surface - only better - it would ensure Tom got through the forest without being seen. Drawing a heavy breath, he stared into Brignar's bulging eyes, then, slowly raising the sword he pointed the tip of the gleaming blade at his chest. 'I will go your way,' he said solemnly. 'But be warned. If you cheat me, I will kill you.'

Brignar smiled as he lifted the scabbard from his back and handed it to Tom. 'Fasten this around your waist, pop the sword back inside and we'll be off. The entrance is just over there.'

A few moments later they were standing by a rocky outcrop at the edge of a wide forest clearing. The air had turned icy cold and Tom was shivering. Badger, still wary of the dwarf, was huddled by his feet.

'Here's the entrance to the tunnel,' Brignar said, pointing to an enormous boulder. Once inside we're safe, but as we're close to Arcos's fortress and the Skrorth are everywhere, keep your eyes trained on the forest while I get this open. Now, give me the sword.'

'No way,' Tom growled. 'The sword stays with me.'

'All right! All right! Keep your voice down. Just do as I say and hurry. Strike the boulder three times then move back.'

As he drew the sword a surge of power again shot through Tom's arm, and when he slammed it down onto the rock, a clanging echo reverberated around the forest.

'Come on,' Brignar whispered as the boulder rumbled open. 'Follow me.'

They entered a narrow passageway, where dancing flames flickered from widely spaced wall torches and the air smelled damp and musty. As the boulder rumbled back into place Brignar hurried away, but just as Tom was about to set off after him, he heard a muffled bark coming from the other side of the stone.

'Wait!' he cried, his voice shrill with alarm. 'Badger's still out there.'

When the dwarf made no response Tom slammed the sword against the stone, but nothing happened.

'Brignar!' he yelled. 'Come back!'

Suddenly, Badger's muffled bark softened to a whimper.

'No!' Tom cried, crashing the sword against the stone over and over again. 'BRIGNAR . . . HOW DO I GET OUT?'

'You mustn't,' the dwarf panted, running back through the gloomy light. 'By now the Skrorth could be everywhere. 'Your dog will be safe. It's not him they want. It's you!'

'Show me how to get out,' Tom screamed, his eyes flaring wide as he raised the sword above Brignar's head. 'Or I swear I'll kill you!'

A strange expression crossed the dwarf's face as he glared at the hovering blade. 'Careful lad,' he whispered.

'Show me!' Tom screamed. 'Or you're dead!'

'All right. All right. Plunge the sword into the stone.'

'That's impossible!'

'If you want your dog, do as I say.'

When Tom thrust the weapon at the boulder a deafening crash echoed around the tunnel, but the blade slipped through the stone like a knife through softened butter. With a loud groan, the boulder rumbled back.

'Be careful,' Brignar whispered.

Clasping the sword with both hands, Tom crept from the tunnel mouth.

'Badger . . . Badger, where are you?'

Then it greeted him. The same foul stench he had encountered in the forest.

'Come back! Skrorth! Don't be foolish.'

Ignoring the dwarf, Tom crept into the open. 'Badger!' he cried, running towards a small, black shape slumped at the base of a withered tree.

The little dog was gasping for breath, a thick, gooey substance covering his face. As a look of panic flashed in his eyes, Tom hurriedly ripped the slime away, scooped Badger into his arms and raced back across the clearing, but as he neared the tunnel mouth he saw a black robed figure blocking his way. Jerking to a sudden stop he slid the sword from its scabbard and thrust the weapon out. As a burst of power pulsed through his veins he edged forward, but as he neared the hissing creature he felt a stinging pain burn his throat, then, as if from nowhere, a thick cloud of purple gas suddenly swirled around his head. It happened so fast he didn't see it coming and as he tried to fight his way through, coughing and spluttering, something hit him right between the eyes. The slimy substance was so thick and gloopy he couldn't pull it off and as it slid down his face, covering his nose and mouth, Tom sank to the ground gasping for breath. As his consciousness began to fade he heard a high-pitched scream followed by a thud, then something grabbed hold of his ankles and started dragging him along the earth. At that moment, everything went black.

When Tom came to, he was back in the tunnel, the inside of his mouth as dry as sandpaper, his stomach churning like a rotating drum. As he eased himself to his knees, blinking to focus his vision, he saw the boulder locked in place across the tunnel mouth. Brignar was standing beside it balancing the powerful, silver sword across his shoulder. He looked ragged and dishevelled, his eyes bulging wide and his body trembling. Badger lay by the dwarf's feet, his paws scratching the earth as he struggled to breathe.

Rising shakily, Tom pulled the wizard's mask from his pocket and hobbling towards Badger, placed it over the little dog's face. 'What happened?' he gasped, as Badger drew hungrily on the clean, fresh air.

The dwarf's face twisted to a grimace. 'I killed the vile creature,' he said, nodding towards the boulder. 'It's out there.' His hands were shaking as he lifted the sword from his shoulder and handed it back to Tom.

'I'm sorry I put you in danger,' Tom said, sliding the weapon back into its scabbard. 'I owe you my life.'

Brignar glared into Tom's eyes, then, without a word, he turned and hurried away. 'You'd best stay close,' he called.

As they moved deeper into the maze of underground tunnels, Tom began to realise that Brignar's encounter with the Skrorth had seriously upset him. The dwarf was now so silent and moody that every time Tom tried to make conversation, he ignored him completely.

After a while they entered an enormous underground cave. Tom felt the clammy air settle like a wet rag on his skin. As they drew to a halt at the centre, he saw several tunnels branching away in different directions. Three of them were lit by wall torches, the others looked dark and gloomy and as he stared into the blackness, he could hear, from somewhere in the distance, a muffled thudding sound.

36

'What's that?' he said, his voice echoing through the stillness.

'It's nothing,' Brignar snapped. 'Just earth sounds.' Pointing to one of the lighted tunnels, he moved towards it. 'We're going through here.'

Tom was beginning to feel a little agitated by Brignar's sullen mood, but knowing he had only the dwarf to rely on, he decided to remain silent.

They threaded their way through a labyrinth of twists and turns and in the sombre atmosphere, where every tunnel looked just like the one before and every turn took them deeper into a complicated maze, a feeling that they were being followed started to grow in Tom's mind. The thought made him jittery and nervous, and every now and then he jerked around to check, but all he could see was the gloomy light from flickering wall torches fading into darkness. I'm being stupid he thought, realising that if anything was lurking in the shadows, Badger would be the first to sense it.

As he trundled on, hoping it would not be long before they emerged into daylight at the other side of the forest, he noticed a gradual slope in the tunnel floor. It was nothing too obvious, just a gentle slant, but nevertheless, it was definitely taking them deeper underground. If they were travelling beneath the Trail of Medioc, surely they would not be moving deeper into the earth. The thought played around in his head for a while, but assuming they were probably just following the natural slope of the land, he decided to ignore it. That was until they came to the top of a steep incline that descended so deep into darkness it looked as though it was leading them into the bowels of the earth.

'Brignar!' Tom called as they started their descent. 'Something's wrong.'

The dwarf, who was a little way ahead, made no reply.

'Brignar! Why don't you answer?'

'I've no desire to talk.' Brignar snapped.

'Well that's too bad,' Tom shouted, jerking to a sudden stop. 'I'm not going any further until you answer me.'

The dwarf slowed his pace and as he halted beneath one of the flickering wall torches, his huge, black shadow crept up the tunnel wall and curved across the ceiling. 'I can't talk and concentrate at the same time. If I talk, I won't remember the way. It's as simple as that.' His bulging eyes rolled towards the darkness ahead. 'Come on, it's not much further. When we get there I'll talk as much as you like.'

Tom felt a twinge of guilt as he watched Brignar shuffle away. The dwarf had after all saved his life, and he had to admit that navigating this confusing labyrinth of tunnels needed a lot of concentration. So, putting his fears behind him, he continued down the slope.

It wasn't long before the ground flattened out and they were once again on a level path, but as they progressed through the dismal light, Tom's niggling doubt that something was wrong refused to go away, and with every step he took, the feeling grew stronger and stronger. He tried to occupy himself by whistling and humming, but eventually he realised that he was not only humming to the rhythm of Brignar's thudding footsteps, his mind was creating its own words: *Something is wrong, something is wrong, thud ump, thud ump, something is wrong.*

'Stop!' he shouted, when he could stand it no longer. But as usual the dwarf ignored him and quickening his pace, disappeared beyond the scope of light. 'Where are you taking me?' Tom yelled, feeling suddenly alone and more vulnerable than ever.

The sound of Brignar's footsteps ceased. Moving back into the glow of a wall torch he shook his head slowly from side to side. 'Where else would I be taking you but to the other side of the forest?'

'I don't know.' Tom shouted. 'But something is wrong.'

Heaving a sigh, the dwarf turned the palms of his outstretched hands upwards and gave a slow, exaggerated shrug. 'You have the sword, why do you worry so?'

'I think we should go back.'

'Go back! We can't go back! By now the Skrorth will be everywhere. I've risked my life for you. I'll not risk it again.'

The last thing Tom wanted was to sound ungrateful, but his instincts were telling him that something bad was about to happen. 'I know you saved me and I know you're trying to help, but something is wrong. I can feel it.'

'We're not going back,' Brignar shrieked, suddenly animated and hostile. 'I won't allow it'

'You won't allow it!' Tom yelled, a flood of anger rising in his throat. 'Then you stay where you are. I'll go on my own.' Swinging around he strode away, but he had taken only a few short strides when a sudden yelp split the silence. Spinning around he saw the dwarf clutching Badger by the scruff of his neck, a gleaming dagger pointed at the little dog's throat.

'You're going nowhere,' Brignar growled.

Without stopping to think, Tom swept the sword from its scabbard and charged.

'I'll split him from top to bottom,' Brignar yelled.

'Why are you doing this?' Tom shrieked, skidding to a halt just inches away.

'Because you my friend are my passage to freedom. When I deliver you to Arcos I will be a hero - one of the chosen ones. Alive, when Keeros and all are dead and gone.'

'But I'm here to stop him,' Tom yelled. 'That's why Altair Devole sent me to get the key. You hate Arcos. You said so!'

'You will never stop him,' Brignar screamed. 'Arcos has more power than you could ever imagine, more evil on his side that you are capable of understanding. This way I am at least assured a life. Now, follow me or your dog dies.'

Standing his ground Tom swung up the sword and glaring into the dwarf's angry eyes he yelled, 'If Badger dies, so do you.'

When Brignar saw his own reflection glinting in the polished steel he erupted into a fit of hysterical laughter, his fat, dumpy body jerking up and down, his eyes flooding with tears. 'With what?' he cried. 'With my sword!' Ha, ha, ha, . . . ha, ha, ha, ha.

Suddenly an evil glare flashed from the dwarf's eyes. Raising the dagger, he leered at Tom as if daring him to strike. But as his wrist jerked back, ready to plunge the blade into Badger's throat, something whizzed past Tom's head, knocking Brignar hard against the tunnel wall. As he slithered to the floor, a silver arrow lodged deep in his chest, a surge of panic shot through Tom. Swinging around he saw a black robed figure standing beneath the glow of a wall torch. 'Skrorth!' he breathed.

A charge of adrenalin suddenly flooded his veins and with a power born from fear he swung the sword up. 'Come on you maggoty piece of septic puss. Come on!'

As he stood their rigid, his thudding heart drumming in his ears, the figure swung the cloak from its shoulders and flung it to the ground. Standing in the dim light was a tall young man with long golden hair. With a yap of instant recognition Badger trotted towards him and as Tom watched in confused disbelief, the little dog ran around the young man's feet, yapping excitedly.

'My name is Lyal.' The stranger smiled. 'And you must be Tom.'

'I thought you were Skrorth.' Tom said, still clasping the sword tightly.

'So did the Skrorth when I passed them in the forest. The disguise fooled them too.'

'How do you know my name?' Tom asked, eyeing the stranger with suspicion. 'And why did you kill the dwarf?'

'Ah,' Lyal said, his deep blue eyes glinting from the light of a wall torch as he moved closer. 'I killed the dwarf because he was trying to capture you. I know your name because Altair Devole told me, and I also know of your mission to retrieve the Charquery Key. What I do not know is why you are here. Did the wizard not bid you to stay on the Trail of Medioc?'

'Yes . . . but . . . Brignar said the Skrorth were waiting in ambush somewhere along the trail . . . he killed one of them and gave me his sword . . . I thought . . . '

'Brignar killed the Skrorth before it could kill you - he needed you alive to negotiate a trade with Arcos. He was leading you to an underground cave where he could keep you prisoner until the time came to exchange you for his freedom. Giving you his sword was a trick to gain your trust.'

'Oh!' Tom sighed, feeling somewhat embarrassed. 'But . . . what are you doing here?'

'I use these tunnels to avoid being seen. I too would be a useful captive to Arcos. When I heard voices I kept out of sight just around that bend. However, when I saw you draw the sword I knew I must stop you. That's when I fired the arrow.'

'I don't understand,' Tom said. 'The dwarf was about to kill Badger. Why would you want to stop me?

'Because of the sword's magic.'

'Magic?'

'If anyone shall try to slay a blue dwarf with his own sword, the weapon shall take to itself the life of the slayer.'

'What?'

'The moment the blade came within a hairs breadth of Brignar it would have swung from your grasp and sliced off your head, leaving the dwarf safely in one piece. His plan was to get you to Arcos alive, but he would have let you die in order to save himself.'

'That's why he laughed when I threatened him?'
'Exactly.'

Swinging the weapon up, Tom gazed at the image of the dwarf still radiating from the gleaming blade. 'Will its magic work for me?' he asked.

'Unfortunately not, only the one who slays a blue dwarf inherits his sword. As the weapon now belongs to me its magic is only potent in my hands. However, as I am now the owner, I can transfer its power to whomever I choose. Give me the sword and I will show you.'

'I'm giving this sword to no one,' Tom shouted, tightening his grip. 'It's mine.'

Lyal remained silent, his gaze fixed on the weapon as if contemplating what to do. Then he suddenly leapt forward, grabbed Tom's wrist and wrenched the sword from his grasp. Ramming the blade into the earth he forced the boy's hand around the hilt and holding it in place, cried: 'Eblis Paebo Anicular.' Tom felt the sword grow hot in his fingers and as a powerful force surged through his body, almost knocking him off his feet, a blinding light shot from the blade.

'The sword takes my strength,' Lyal gasped, sliding to his knees. 'Its power . . . its magic, , , is now yours.'

As his grip fell loose Tom was catapulted against the tunnel wall. Stunned and trembling he watched the sword swaying from side to side and when his eyes focused on the blade, he saw the image of the blue dwarf fading, slowly transforming into an image of himself.

I'm sorry I startled you,' Lyal said, helping Tom to his feet. 'But it had to be that way. You would never have given up the sword willingly and there was not enough time to try to convince you. The sword now belongs to you - it holds your image. No one will be able to use it against you. If they do, they will die.' Smiling, he slid the weapon back into the scabbard at Tom's side. 'Now my friend, you must return to Bragenon.'

'Bragenon!' Tom exclaimed. 'But the Skrorth are waiting in ambush. I'll never get through the forest?'

'Skrorth are stupid creatures and easy to fool. A short while ago I travelled through Bragenon in disguise.' Plucking the robe from the ground, Lyal ripped a broad piece of cloth from the bottom then swirled the garment around Tom's shoulders. 'As long as you look like one of them and do not arouse suspicion, they will not know the difference.' Pulling the hood down over Tom's face, he then concealed each of his hands in the broad width of sleeve, until nothing of him could be seen. 'You look perfect,' he grinned.

'But I'm too small,' Tom exclaimed. 'The Skrorth I saw was tall like you.'

'They're not all alike. Some are taller than me and some are smaller than you. Don't worry, you're just right. Come, we must hurry.'

With Badger racing ahead, they headed back through the complicated maze of tunnels until they reached the underground cave, where a muffled thudding sound still echoed from the distance. 'Where's that noise coming from,' Tom asked, pulling to a stop at the centre.

'The sound you hear comes from the blue dwarves of Bragenon. They are few in number, and until Arcos opened the Pit of Pendurak they lived in the forest. When Bragenon began to die, they took refuge underground where they set about restoring an abandoned forge, which they are using to

44

make weapons of war. When the time comes for Arcos and his evil followers to invade your world, they will be ready to go with him. However, they need a reason to get Arcos to agree. Brignar, their leader, knew that sooner or later someone would try to reach Delnar to seek help from the element of fire. Certain no one would enter Bragenon for any other purpose, he devised a plan to capture whoever came this way. Once his captive was in chains, he could negotiate a trade with Arcos in return for safe passage to earth.'

'Whew,' Tom breathed, 'I guess I'm lucky you were in the tunnel when I needed help.'

When they arrived at the boulder, Lyal pulled a white mask from his tunic and handed it to Tom. 'After you left the Abalon Tree, the wizard realised he should have given you two of these - one for you and one for Badger. 'Bending down he gently secured the mask around the little dog's head. 'You'd better put yours on before you enter the forest.'

When Tom's mask was firmly in position, Lyal placed Badger in his arms. 'Carry him inside the cloak until you are safely out of Bragenon. When you leave the tunnel you will see a trail of white pebbles. Follow them until you reach the place where you met the dwarf, then continue along the trail to the other side of the forest.' Placing his hand firmly on Tom's shoulder he said, 'You have learnt a hard lesson my friend. Do not be diverted again.'

'But the ambush,' Tom said. 'What if . . . ?'

'Should you encounter Skrorth, be sure keep well hidden beneath the cloak. Stay calm, and above all do not try to speak. They have no words - they use gestures and movement to relay their thoughts. It is vital you behave like one of them until you are able to leave their presence without arousing suspicion. It's the only way.'

Placing his hand on the boulder, Lyal mumbled a string of words Tom did not understand. 'I can go no further,' he said as the rock rumbled open. 'From here you are on your own. Be sure to keep the sword with you at all times.'

Tom detected the putrid stench of Skrorth as soon as he moved into the open. Looking down, he saw the creature Brignar had killed sprawled on the ground close to the tunnel entrance. The body was completely covered by the folds of its long, black cloak, except for a wizened hand jutting from one of the sleeves. Tom shuddered at the sight of the deep red talons curling from the ends of its clawed fingers and felt his stomach turn when he noticed little volcanoes of purple slime erupting from the slippery, mottled skin.

Holding his breath, he carefully picked his way around it, then quickening his step, made his way along the trail of white pebbles. When he reached the spot where he had first encountered the blue dwarf he turned onto the trail, shuddering at the sound of his footsteps crunching the frosty earth. To him they seemed as loud as gunfire in a tunnel.

With his vision partially blocked by the hooded robe, Tom was unable to see between the trees on either side of the track - a situation that made him feel nervous and edgy, so he hurried along with one hand holding Badger and the other gripped tight around the hilt of his sword. Eventually, after navigating a series of snaking bends, he arrived at the bottom of a steep slope. Glancing upwards, making sure his face could not be seen, he saw the trail disappear into darkness through a huddle of wizened trees. The climb was not easy to navigate with the cloak flapping around his ankles and after stumbling several times, he was tempted to throw it off and make a run for it. As it turned out, that would have been a big mistake, because at that moment he heard a low growl rumble in Badger's throat.

He slowed almost to a stop, raised his head just enough to see without being seen and moving slowly forward, one nervous step after another, came to the top of the rise. Then he stopped dead, his heart thudding as a whip of fear snaked down his spine. A black robed figure was moving straight towards him.

With his mind screaming fear he tried desperately to think of what to do. Should he stop? Should he continue? Then he suddenly remembered Lyal's words. *'Should you encounter Skrorth stay calm, and above all do not try to speak. They have no words. They use gestures and movement to relay their thoughts.'*

As the creature drew near it pulled to a stop, then a grey, mottled hand slid from the sleeve of its robe and beckoned. *'You must behave like one of them until you can leave their presence without arousing suspicion.'*

Tom edged slowly forward, his teeth clamped tight to stop them from chattering. When he was that close to the Skrorth he could smell the sickening stench of its being, he held his breath, certain that at any moment he would be discovered. But the creature merely beckoned again, then turning, started to move away.

He followed it to the edge of the trail where it slid out of sight behind one of the withered trees. Tom did exactly the same, his cold, clammy hands weak and trembling. Turning his head as far as he dared he peered from under his hood. He could see about ten of them hiding in the trees.

He stood there for a long time hardly daring to breathe, silently praying that Badger would not make a sound. Nothing moved. Nothing spoke. Only stillness and fear filled the air. Tom knew that he must return the Charquery Key before the end of equinox and as time ticked slowly by, he felt the success of his mission slipping further and further away. Though Lyal had told him to do nothing until it was safe, he knew he would soon have to act. He had no alternative but to try to escape. Turning slowly, raising his head just enough to peer beneath his hood, he carefully examined the surrounding woodland. He could dart between the trees, run like the wind and hope against hope he could outrun them.

As he stood there pondering his chances, a high pitched screech suddenly blasted the silence, like the ear piercing scream of metal grinding against metal. The Skrorth responded instantly. As if obeying a command, they moved one by one onto the trail, forming a single black line along its centre. Tom held back, hoping when they had all gone he could slip away unnoticed. But that was not going to happen. When the time came for the two closest to him to move, they swung towards him, expecting him to follow.

With his skin hot and sweaty and his body trembling, he followed them to the rear of the line, taking a position at the very end, where the stench of Skrorth was so strong it made him want to throw up. Suddenly another convulsion of fiendish notes rang out. The silent black line responded at once, turning one by one onto the forest. As Tom entered the trees he felt the gloom of Bragenon enfold him and the fear of not knowing where he was going started gnawing at his brain. He must do something . . . but what?

They hadn't gone far when the Skrorth started filtering off to the right, disappearing one by one behind a dilapidated stone wall surrounding the ruins of an ancient castle. Slowing his pace, Tom let a gap to form between himself and the creature in front, and in case any of them looked back, he padded his feet up and down to make it look like he was still moving.

When the last of the Skrorth vanished from sight he flung off the cloak, put Badger on the ground, and with their masks still tied around their faces, they raced through the forest like fleeing convicts.

When they reached the Trail of Medioc, Tom took a flying leap onto the path, but as his feet thudded down, something hard hit him in the back. He crashed to the ground and flinging out his arms to break his fall, saw a hissing black mass hurtling towards him. With no time to think he rolled across the earth, slid the sword from its scabbard and as the charging Skrorth lunged, he thrust the weapon out. The creature staggered back, a cloud of purple gas suddenly billowing from its hood, growing thicker and thicker until it could no longer be seen. Springing to his feet, Tom swung his sword from left to right, pushing clumsily through the choking haze. He could hear Badger barking. He could sense movement behind. Spinning around, he sliced the sword in a wide arc as he turned . . . Thud! Through the thinning mist he saw the Skrorth staggering towards him, a gush of warm liquid oozing from a deep wound in its chest. The creature suddenly faltered and shuddering violently sank to its knees, then its head, covered by swirls of twisted black cloth, toppled from its shoulders.

Taken by a sudden fit of panic, Tom rammed the sword back into its scabbard. Running so fast his feet barely touched the ground he felt a rush of terror course through his veins, making everything seem unreal, everything a threat. Smudges of blackened trees whizzed by - malevolent shapes ready to snatch him from the earth. He ran and he ran and he ran, until finally, when his breath gave out and he could run no more, he collapsed in a heap on the ground. Clutching at the sharp pain gripping his side, he lay there gasping, praying he had not been followed.

50

When he finally managed to pull himself up, he saw Badger sprawled by his feet panting. He peered along the trail, his gaze darting fearfully through the trees in search of Skrorth. But the forest was still and silent. Rising to his feet, he lifted Badger into his arms and hugged him close. 'Let's hope that's the last we see of them,' he whispered.

The remainder of their journey was uneventful and when at last they reached the other side of Bragenon, they moved from the dark, dismal gloom into an explosion of dazzling sunlight. 'We've made it!' Tom yelled, grinning from ear to ear as he yanked Badger's mask off and slid it, along with his own, into his pocket.

They were standing at the top of a steep slope. Stretching out below them was a wide expanse of grassland peppered with copper tinted trees and swathes of colourful wild flowers. In the distance, a lopsided mountain slumped like a snoozing giant against the clear blue sky, its base surrounded by a ridge of dense woodland. Poking from the centre of the trees were the turrets and towers of an ancient gothic castle.

To make sure he was heading in the right direction, Tom pulled the wizard's map from his sock, stretched it out on the ground then ran his finger across the parchment to the spot where the trail of Medioc split into two separate tracks. The path to the right - the one he must follow - led to a large flat-topped boulder displaying the imprint of a shoe. Carved into the side of the stone were the words, *Kingdom of the Festinol.* Suddenly remembering he had lost the wizard's shoe in the river - the shoe that was to gain him entry to the kingdom - he sighed heavily, wondering how he would get in. Then he slid his finger along the other path, following it to the edge of the page. Neither the mountain nor the castle was illustrated. Shrugging, he folded the map and returned it to his sock.

51

As he rose to his feet he saw Badger scratching furiously at the earth. 'What are you doing?' he shouted. Suddenly, as if being bitten by some vicious creature, the little dog yelped and jerked back. Then his body turned as stiff and rigid as a statue. 'Badger! What's wrong! Rushing towards him Tom fell to his knees. He slid his hand along the little dog's back, stroked the fur under his chin. But Badger didn't move, his eyes were as vacant as two glass marbles. 'Badger, what is it?' Then he noticed a hole about the size of a small rabbit burrow close to Badger's feet.

Leaning forward he peered inside. He could smell something strange. Moving his hand to the edge of the hole he leaned down further. Suddenly, something wet and cold squirted into his face. Leaping to his feet he swayed from side to side as a paralysing weakness swept through him. He felt his heartbeat slow down, his breathing turns shallow, and when he tried to move his legs they wouldn't budge. Then, through the blurry haze clouding his vision he saw an enormous snake slither from the hole.

The serpent rose up until its head was directly in line with Tom's face. He could feel the cold hiss of its breath on his skin. Unable to move he watched it sway slowly from side to side, its forked tongue lashing in and out, its bright, orange eyes glaring directly into his. All of a sudden it coiled like a corkscrew and started spinning around and round, turning faster and faster until Tom could see nothing but a blur of whirling dust. Then, as suddenly as it had begun, the whirling motion ceased, the dust cloud settled, and standing there before him was a strange looking creature. It had the body of a man, the head of a snake and was dressed in a garment covered with glistening silver scales.

'I am Scavrad,' it hissed. 'Master of the kill.'

The creature circled Tom slowly, all the while its putrid breath falling like poisoned mist onto his skin. 'I can hold you in my power for as long as I wish. Or I can kill you slowly, painfully, ling . . er . . ing . . ly.' As the creature's head drew back, two curved fangs sprang from the roof of its mouth, tiny drops of venom dripping from the tips. 'However,' it grinned, slowly retracting the poisonous weapons of death. 'I will show you mercy. For the moment I will release you. But take heed. Any attempt to escape and you are dead.'

As a silvery membrane swept across the snake man's orange eyes, Tom felt a flush of warmth sweep through him. As soon as he could move he ran to Badger. 'Let him go!' he yelled, sliding his hand along the little dog's rigid body.

'You are in no position to command,' the creature hissed.

'Please release him. Whatever it is you want I will do, if only you let him go.'

'You will do what I want whether I release him or not. You have no choice.'

'Yes I have!' Swinging around, Tom grabbed the hilt of his sword, but before he could fully draw the blade, something cold hit the back of his hand. His arm instantly locked, he couldn't move his wrist and his fingers felt as though they were turning to stone.

'The dog stays,' Scavrad roared. 'You will come with me.'

'Why?' Tom shouted. 'What do you want?'

'I want whatever will please the master. We creatures of Pendurak serve him well.'

While being forced back into the dismal gloom of Bragenon, Tom swung around to take a final look at Badger. The little dog looked so helpless, like a tiny lifeless statue staring out across the grassy plain, and the thought of leaving him there all alone made Tom feel sick inside.

When the numbness left his hand, he pushed the sword, which was still half drawn, down into its scabbard - a movement that triggered a swift response from the snake man. Grabbing him by the hair, Scavrad swung him round. 'Take care,' he hissed, jabbing Tom hard in the chest. 'One false move and you are dead.' Tom glared at him coldly, revulsion radiating from his eyes as his fingers tightened around the hilt of his sword. All he wanted was to slice the vile creature's head clean off. But he knew he wouldn't stand a chance. Instead he turned and walked away.

They continued through the forest in silence and when Tom saw the ground turning white with frost, he knew they were drawing closer to Arcos's fortress. Eventually he felt a blast of cold air sting his skin. Peering ahead, through the dwindling number of withered trees, he saw a colossal wall of ice curving away in both directions. At the centre of the wall stood a narrow tunnel guarded by two enormous creatures. Though their bodies resembled those of huge, muscular dogs, their heads, surrounded by manes of black, matted fur, were unlike anything Tom had ever seen. Huge tusks bulged from either side of their heavy, salivating jaws, thick, curved fangs protruded from their drooling, fleshy mouths and their bulging yellow eyes had stark, red lines radiating from the centre.

'Grybb,' Scavrad hissed, 'one of our more endearing creatures. Come . . . we must pass between them.'

When the dogs spotted Tom they leapt across the ice howling like ravenous wolves, but suddenly yanked back by the heavy metal chains hanging around their throats, they thudded to the ground yelping and growling. Panicked by the thought of getting any closer, Tom wedged his feet firmly into the earth and refused to move.

'Fear not,' Scavrad sniggered. 'Watch!'

With lightning speed, he lunged at one of the beasts, his deadly fangs dripping venom, his eyes glaring wide. With a yelp of fear the creature cowered to the ground, cringing and whimpering like a frightened puppy. The other retreated to the wall.

'I am Master of the kill,' the snake man screamed, forcing Tom between the trembling Grybb. 'No one but Arcos has more power than I. No one!'

Tom followed the swaggering snake man through the ice tunnel, emerging from the other side at the edge of an enormous circular enclosure. At its centre an assortment of grotesque creatures were gathered around a smoking pit, their eyes riveted on a black cloud hovering above their heads. The stench was so awful it made Tom's stomach turn.

To the right, and in stark contrast to its surroundings, stood a glistening palace made entirely of ice. Figures of angels and cherubs were positioned around the walls in such a way they looked as if they were clambering towards the parapets, where water cascading from huge, grotesque gargoyles poured clouds of white spray into the freezing air. At each corner of the palace stood a rectangular watchtower and though each one was occupied by a dark, sinister shape, it was impossible for Tom to distinguish what they were.

Suddenly an ear-splitting screech came from the direction of the pit. When Tom swung around he saw a weird, goblin-like creature leaping up and down pointing in his direction. The rest of the fiendish mob looked up and erupting in an explosion of squeaks and squeals, turned in Tom's direction and stampeded across the ice towards him.

Scavrad moved forward, his orange eyes glaring as the unruly crowd crashed and bashed each other as they skidded to a halt. Swaggering before them, his glistening fangs dripping venom, he yelled. 'Go tell the master it is I, Scavrad who brings the prize.' But the inquisitive creatures - their bloodthirsty eyes boring into Tom like knives - refused to move. 'Go!' the snake man screamed. 'Or one of you will die!' When he suddenly lunged forward, the mob jolted back, then, swinging around in a wave of panic, they raced back towards the pit.

'Pendurak,' Scavrad hissed, watching the crowd gather beneath the hovering black cloud. 'As long as Arcos holds Pendurak's power he is invincible. Soon he will lead us through the gateway to earth, a conqueror in all his glory. And you . . .' he prodded a bony finger hard into Tom's shoulder '. . . will never be allowed to stop us.'

While the snake man strutted back and forth proclaiming his greatness Tom's eyes scanned the ice wall searching for another exit - one that may not be as well guarded as the tunnel. He saw clusters of ice shelters resembling miniature igloos edging the perimeter of the enclosure, but there were no other openings. Turning his attention to the pit, he saw that the billowing green smoke had subsided to a thin, shallow mist. Through it, at the other side of the gaping hole, he saw a huge column of ice with a glistening object lodged at its centre. As he squeezed his eyes, trying to make out what the object could be, a clap of thunder rumbled across the sky.

The chanting crowd of demons fell silent and dropping to their knees, watched in awe as a glistening silver orb slid from the black cloud hovering above them. It moved slowly across the encampment and when it drew close to where Tom was standing, it floated to the ground as lightly as a bubble of soap. Blinded by the glare, Tom thrust his hands in front of his eyes and peering through his fingers, watched in astonishment as a tall, silver haired figure emerged from the orb. He gasped when he saw the creature's strikingly handsome face, which looked as if it had been sculpted out of pure crystal. As it moved towards him, its dazzling white robes billowing on the breeze, Tom felt a blast of arctic wind slice through his body, and sensed a power so awesome it took his breath away. 'Arcos!' he whispered, as a sharp pain shot between his temples and a noise like the drumming of a pulse rattled in his brain.

'So you are the one sent to challenge my power,' the ice man sneered. 'You have done well Scavrad. For this you will be rewarded. But first, we must show our guest the fate of those who displease us. Bring him!' As Arcos swept away Tom was seized by two horned gremlins who hauled him across the ice towards the glistening white palace, where he was thrown to the ground at the ice man's feet.

The fiendish crowd of imps and goblins were now clustered like cave bats at the other side of the pit. When a line of black robed figures, flanked on either side by gigantic lizard headed guards, emerged from the rear of the ice palace, they leapt up and down, yelping and whooping with excitement.

57

'You failed!' Arcos roared, as the Skrorth were lined up before him. Swinging around he glared at the boisterous mob, which immediately fell silent. 'Let this be a lesson to you all,' he yelled. 'If you fail me you will be punished.' Thrusting a clenched fist into the air he swung towards the ice palace, his voice resonating around the enclosure as he screamed a command. Suddenly a pack of howling Grybb, like those guarding the tunnel, bounded towards him. 'This is your reward for failure,' he bellowed, pointing at the Skrorth. 'From Pendurak you were freed. To Pendurak you will return. Dishonoured and discarded forever.'

On his signal the Grybb encircled the Skrorth and crouching like stalking lions, crept towards their prey. But the Skrorth were powerful adversaries, capable of despatching any one the beasts with ease. Moving together they formed a tight circle and as clouds of deadly gas billowed from beneath their hoods, they swung around to face their attackers.

The largest of the beasts leapt from the ground and seizing one of the Skrorth by the shoulder, sank its razor sharp fangs deep into the hissing creature's flesh. As the Skrorth's hood fell back, revealing a throbbing mass of mottled, pulsating flesh, its eyes suddenly flamed like two burning orbs. Then, without warning, a jet of thick, green liquid shot from its mouth, quickly spreading over the Grybb's head like butter on hot toast. Squealing with terror the beast pawed at its face, but the liquid was turning to sticky, suffocating slime and the more it struggled, the harder the stuff set. As the other Grybb watched in petrified silence, the Skrorth grabbed the terrified creature by the scruff of its neck and in spite of its size, tossed it into the air, spinning it round until it was completely cocooned in a tangle of sticky, green slime. Then it flung the immobilized beast to the ground where it writhed and struggled like a fly trapped in a web.

Soon every single Grybb had been disposed of in this way and after the last had been incarcerated, the band of Skrorth closed together in victory. Arcos, who had been watching the performance with a degree of amusement, turned to a column of burly, lizard-headed guards. At his signal they thundered forward, their huge clawed feet booming across the ice, their fat, lizard tails crashing from side to side. When they reached the Grybb, they ripped the slime from each of their faces then moved in a tightly controlled line towards the Skrorth. As they approached, a cloud of deadly gas enveloped them, but immune to its poison they kept pushing forward, forcing their hissing adversaries to the very edge of the pit.

Hovering on the brink, the Skrorth spat like wildcats, slashing at the lizard heads with their razor sharp talons. But it was no use, one by one they were bulldozed over the edge, plunging like screeching banshees into the stinking hole. When the last of them had gone there was a belch of green smoke, a gurgle of displaced slime, then silence.

As the bullheads retreated, Arcos strode away in the direction of the ice palace, while Scavrad, following his master's orders, frog marched Tom to where the boisterous crowd of demons were gathered at the other side of the pit.

'I am summoned to the master,' he cried, tying Tom to the trunk of a withered tree. 'Take care of our guest while I am gone. But be warned. If any one of you harms him, they will answer to me. He is mine.'

As he turned to leave, a thickset, muscular creature with a broad bull's head and curved, serrated horns thundered from the crowd and barred his way. 'Why yours?' it grunted, confronting the snake man with a challenging glare. 'What makes you so special?'

Scavrad grinned menacingly. Then his hypnotic eyes drilled into the bullheads like two burning spikes. The creature, locked in a mesmerising glare found it impossible to look away and as the snake man swayed from side to side, so did the bullhead. As fear coursed through its veins its skin turned icy cold and when Scavrad glared deeper into its eyes, its body grew weak and heavy. It tried to move its legs, tried to swing its powerful horns, but frozen beneath the snake man's spellbinding gaze, it couldn't move a muscle.

'I am Master of the Kill,' Scavrad hissed, circling the bullhead slowly. 'When the time comes, it is I who will have the honour of dispensing with the boy, I who will fill his blood with poison until he writhes in agony.' As two dripping fangs sprang from the sides of the snake man's mouth he glared into the bullhead's startled eyes. Then he suddenly shot forward as if to strike. 'Let this be a lesson,' he breathed, stopping short of the creature's neck. 'This time I will show you mercy . . . Challenge me again and you will die!' As soon as he released it the petrified creature dived headlong into the watching crowd.

'I am Master of the Kill.' Scavrad screamed again. 'If anyone harms my prize they will die!' With that, he hurried away in the direction of the ice palace.

When the snake man was safely out of sight, the fiendish collection of ghouls and gremlins closed in, their excited voices chittering and screeching like a pack of hungry vultures. Suddenly a trio of aggressive looking goblins with bulbous black eyes and slimy wrinkled skin forced their way to the front. They pushed their grotesque faces right up to Tom's and when he tried to turn away they leapt about screeching and yowling like a troupe of demented monkeys. Then each in turn slid its slimy fingers around his throat,

60

squeezing so hard, his face turned red and his eyes began to bulge.

The defeated bullhead, afraid it might be blamed if Tom was harmed, suddenly charged from the centre of the crowd and bulldozing his tormentors out of the way, flung them one by one to the ground. Towering above them, roaring with fury, it glared at each in turn, daring them to retaliate. But the terrified goblins, quaking with fear, scrambled to their feet as fast as they could and scurried away.

As the bullhead stomped up and down, swaggering arrogantly before the cheering crowd, it noticed something glint in the corner of its eye. Thudding to a halt it swung around, its huge, muscular body causing the ice beneath its feet to crack. Tom felt a rush of fear as its probing eyes glared at his face, then its gaze suddenly dropped to the sword strapped to his side. The creature glanced nervously from left too right, peered across the encampment towards the ice palace. Satisfied Arcos and Scavrad were nowhere in sight, it drew a deep, shuddering breath, rushed forward and yanked the weapon from its scabbard.

As a jolt of power surged through the creature's arm it glared into the gleaming blade, its eyes growing wide with astonishment. Then, squealing like an excited child it started slicing the air, sweeping the weapon backwards and forwards over the heads of the startled crowd. In a desperate attempt to divert the crazed bullhead's attention, one of the petrified spectators jabbed a clawed finger in Tom's direction, shouting: 'Chop off 'is 'ed! Chop off 'is 'ed! Why should Scavrad 'av all the fun?'

'We needn't be afraid if we all stick together,' screamed another. 'He can't kill us all.'

61

Suddenly the crowd rose to their feet and chanting in unison cried, 'Chop off 'is 'ed. Chop off 'is 'ed. Chop off 'is ed.'

'We must ask the master, a lone voice cried. 'We answer to him.' But the voice was instantly silenced.

Bolstered by the mob, crazed by the force surging through its veins, the bullhead thrust the sword into the air, sweeping it wildly from side to side. 'I answer to no one,' it roared. 'I answer to no one.'

At that moment a blinding flash illuminated the sky. As the petrified crowd fell to their knees, Arcos appeared before them, his white robes swirling, his face alive with fury. 'You answer to me,' he screamed, his voice resonating around the encampment.

The startled bullhead froze, its glassy eyes almost bursting from their sockets. Then it suddenly flung the sword to the ground and screeching like a demented chimpanzee, bolted for the ice tunnel.

'I will capture the traitor.' Scavrad yelled, racing across the enclosure towards the ice man. 'Leave him to me.'

'No' Arcos barked. 'The beasts must have their fill.' Pulling a set of silver pipes from his tunic he placed them to his lips. The same spine chilling sound Tom had heard in the forest blasted across the encampment. Suddenly a pack of snarling Grybb came tearing from the rear of the ice palace and guided by the unmelodious notes of command, sped towards the tunnel. Within moments the bullhead's agonised screams rang from the forest.

Arcos moved to the edge of the pit and thrusting his arms in the air, bellowed into its murky depths. As a cloud of green smoke gushed from the abyss hundreds of ghostly forms rose up to greet him, swaying and swirling in the shadowy haze. 'The dark secrets of the universe will soon be mine,' he yelled. 'Mine to command!' As he turned to the startled mob, his eyes glinting madly, they bowed down before him, their voices rising to fever pitch as they chanted, 'Arcos, Arcos, Arcos.'

When Tom lowered his head, sickened by the chilling display, he saw the sword, which had been flung down by the bullhead, lying on the ground close to his feet. He glanced cautiously at the unruly mob - who were now listening intently to what Arcos was saying - then, stretching his body as far as he could, he pushed his leg out. He wriggled the toe of his shoe, trying to catch the tip of the blade. 'Ugh!' he sighed when his shoe caught the edge of the sword and pushed it further away. In frustration he tugged at his wrists, trying to slacken the tethers, but they were tied so tight that every time he pulled, a searing pain shot through his arms. After several attempts he felt a trickle of warm blood run down his fingers. There was no way he was going to escape.

Hearing an unearthly screech resonated around the enclosure he felt the chill of hopelessness wash over him. Slumping back against the tree he closed his eyes and thought of Badger stranded alone at the edge of the dark forest.

CHAPTER 6

While Tom was locked deep in thought, convinced he was trapped in some strange, nightmarish dream, he suddenly sensed a presence. Opening his eyes, he saw Scavrad glaring down at him, swinging the gleaming silver sword.

'You think you can stop me with this?' the snake man hissed, glaring contemptuously at the shimmering blade. 'This piece of junk has no power here. And to prove how useless it is . . . I will let you have it back.' Untying Tom's wrists, smirking as he watched him rise shakily to his feet, he slid the weapon back into its scabbard. 'Try using it!' he grinned. 'I dare you!'

On Scavrad's command, two hefty gremlins grabbed hold of Tom's arms and dragged him towards the smouldering pit, where Arcos and his band of screeching demons were gathered. The hostile crowd danced about excitedly and as Tom was forced between them, they sneered and snickered, poked and prodded, jabbed their clawed fingers at the pit, itching to throw him in.

Arcos, whose face reflected an aura of enjoyment, was standing close to the edge, calmly inhaling the putrid vapours. 'What I don't understand,' he said, when Tom was hauled before him, 'is why they sent a child to do the work of wizards?' His cold, penetrating eyes swept from the top of Tom's head to the tips of his toes and back again. 'Ah! I see. They thought I would not suspect a boy. Well they were wrong!' As his icy words lingered on the air, his face contorted to a menacing smile. 'Come,' he said, beckoning a long, crystalline finger. 'Let us show you the thing for which you came - the most important object ever created. It is only fair to allow you a glimpse before you die.'

Tom was frog-marched to the other side of the pit, where a column of ice - so tall it could be seen from anywhere in the encampment towered from the ground. At its centre sat a glistening silver key. 'There is your prize,' Arcos grinned. 'The Charquery Key. Take a good, long look, for this is the closest you will ever come.' Swinging around he glared angrily at Scavrad. 'What were they thinking of sending a boy? Am I worth no more than that?'

'They insult you master!' Scavrad shrieked. 'Let me rid you of this gross humiliation. Let me have my reward for delivering the boy into your hands.'

'Ah yes.' Arcos breathed. 'Your reward . . . I almost forgot.' As he turned back to Tom, grinning menacingly, he spotted the sword strapped around the boy's waist. 'And what do we have here?' he grinned.

With slow deliberation, he slid the weapon from its scabbard, glaring, with some degree of amusement, into its shimmering blade. 'They thought you could defeat me with this puny piece of metal? Scavrad is right. They do insult me, they do humiliate me. How dare they?' Grinning coldly, he pointed the razor sharp blade at Tom's throat. 'I could slice off your head with one swipe. In fact . . . I think I will.'

Tom's heart began to race and as Arcos raised the sword high above his head, he remembered Lyal's words: *'If anyone should try to slay a blue dwarf with his own sword, it will take to itself the life of the slayer. Now the sword is yours, for you it holds the same power.'*

When Arcos swung the weapon back, a deathly silence descended on the encampment. As the swish of metal sliced

65

through the air, Tom squeezed his eyes, praying the sword's magic would work. But Arcos swept the blade high over Tom's head, his sinister laugh ringing through the silence. 'See how he trembles and quakes,' he roared. 'How dare they send a boy to do the work of wizards?' Pushing the sword forcibly into Scavrad's hand, he glared into the snake man's eyes. 'Take your reward. But you must kill him with this - the weapon they chose to defeat me with. And when you are done, you will return his sword, and his head, to the Eastern wizard.'

'But master . . . I . . . '

Scavrad found it hard to conceal his disappointment. To him the sword was clumsy and unrefined - a weapon of mortal men. He would much rather savour a lingering, painful death than merely slice off someone's head. But he knew only too well the price he would pay for defying Arcos. The master had spoken. He must be obeyed.

'Not the way I would choose master,' he grimaced, curving his thin, reptilian mouth into an obsequious grin. 'But good enough!'

'No!' Tom suddenly shrieked, glaring at Arcos. 'You do it! Strike the blow yourself. If you dare!'

Arcos's eyes suddenly flared with rage. Snatching the sword from Scavrad, he strode up to Tom and screamed, 'You have the nerve to challenge me? You dare question my power?'

'You're a coward,' Tom yelled, 'who uses others to perform his evil deeds. Strike the blow yourself. Let your true power be seen. I dare you!'

'You promised master,' Scavrad squealed as Arcos clenched the sword in both hands and raised it in line with Tom's neck. 'My reward! You promised!'

Lowering his shaking arms Arcos brought the weapon to his side and leaning down until his face was directly in line with Tom's, whispered, 'Your courage I admire. For this I allow you to irritate me. But make no mistake. I am more than capable of killing you - and I need no scrawny piece of metal to do it. Watch!'

As he swung towards the crowd, they huddled together like frightened sheep. Grinning sadistically, he pointed to an aggressive looking demon with fiery, red eyes and sharp pointed teeth. When he beckoned, the creature shuddered with fright and turning to the others, tried to squeeze between them, but they grabbed it by the arms and pushed it forward, thankful the master had not chosen one of them.

The demon advanced with jerky, faltering steps, its gangly limbs twitching and shuddering while bursts of fiery red sparks spluttered nervously from its mouth. As it drew close to Arcos, cringing with fear, he grinned maliciously. Stepping back, the ice man slowly raised his hand and when it was in line with the demon's head, an explosion of radiant beams shot from the ends of his long, crystalline fingers. Criss-crossing in all directions they surrounded the terrified creature until it was completely encased in a cage of dazzling light. As its eyes bulged with fear, its skin started to glow, the colour rapidly draining as it swung back and forth like a worm trapped in sunlight. Then it suddenly let out an ear piercing scream, bolted upright and turned to solid ice. A fearful murmur rose from the crowd as the ice started to crack. Bit by bit it snapped and splintered, then all at once the creature shattered into thousands of tiny pieces.

'I need no scrawny piece of metal to display my power,' Arcos screamed as he thrust the sword at Scavrad. 'Take off his head!'

'Kill him. Kill him. Kill him,' the mob chanted.

Grinning triumphantly Scavrad swung the weapon back, pausing for just a moment to savour the look of horror in Tom's startled eyes. Then he swept it round with every ounce of strength he could muster. But when the blade came within an inch of Tom's neck it shuddered to a stop. There was a blinding flash, a buzz of fear. As if having a mind of its own, the sword wrenched itself from the snake man's grasp, whipped through the air with heavy, slicing thrusts and chopped his astonished head clean off his body.

'What trickery is this?' Arcos yelled when the sword rammed itself back into the scabbard at Tom's side. 'What foul trickery is this?' As he glared in horror at Scavrad's decapitated body the startled crowd stampeded towards him, rapidly surrounding him in a scuffle of fear and confusion.

At that moment, while the ice man was distracted, Tom seized his chance. Pushing through the swell of tangled bodies he raced to the ice block, and in an attempt to release the key, started hacking away with the blood spattered sword. But the ice was indestructible, the sword had no effect, and no matter how hard he tried, he couldn't chip away even a splinter. Suddenly the boom of Arcos's voice resonated around the enclosure. 'Finish him,' he bellowed.

The panic stricken mob swung around. Screaming for blood they charged at Tom like a pack of ravenous wildcats. They were almost upon him, ready to tear him limb from limb, when an ear-splitting screech echoed across the sky. The crazed mob looked up and gasping in horror saw the enormous Skrell plunging down towards them. Besieged with panic they stumbled back to their master, shrieking and screaming as the massive predator swooped over their heads. When it reached the ice block it grabbed Tom by the shoulders and swept him away.

All he could hear as he was dragged across the sky was the waft of powerful wings beating overhead. The bird was flying at tremendous speed and as a rush of icy wind pushed against his body, the sword, which he was still clasping tight in his hand, started shuddering violently. Fearing it was about to be wrenched away, he forced the blade around and rammed it hard into its scabbard. Then, as he watched the Skrell's black shadow sweep over a blur of undulating grassland, his stomach suddenly lurched, his arms shot over his head and his breath caught sharp in the back of his throat. The bird had begun its descent.

Hurtling towards the ground he saw the contours of the landscape rise up to meet him and certain he was about to be spattered into the earth, he squeezed his eyes shut. But the Skrell suddenly slowed, hovered above a wide mound of grass and released its grip. Hitting the ground with a gentle thud, Tom quickly scrambled to his feet. As he watched the bird lumber to a halt he tried to draw his sword, but his fingers were so numb with cold they wouldn't bend. In desperation he turned to run. His legs were as stiff as two frozen planks and when he tried to put one foot in front of the other, he collapsed in a heap on the ground. Powerless to defend himself he did the only thing he could think of. He turned onto his stomach, curled into a ball and shielded his head with his hands. Trembling with fear he closed his eyes, waiting for the predators tearing talons.

Suddenly a loud bang shattered the silence. Tom jumped, his hands shot over his ears and from the corner of his eye he

69

saw a blur of movement. He turned his head slowly, his body trembling, his mouth dropping open as he let out a startled cry. The Skrell was shimmering like a mirage, its body glowing incandescently. Then all of a sudden it vanished, and there, surrounded by a bright, glowing aura, stood Lyal.

Tom was so shocked he could barely move, his face a mask of white. 'Where did you come from?' he whispered. 'Where's the Skrell?'

'I am the Skrell!' Lyal smiled. 'And you my friend are a very difficult person to save.'

'Save!' Tom exclaimed as he scrambled to his feet. 'I thought the Skrell was trying to kill me!'

Before Lyal could answer a blood curdling howl rang from the distance. 'There's no time to explain,' he said, 'the Grybb are sent to kill you. Go before they catch your scent.' He pointed to a dusty track winding away across a stretch of open grassland. 'You must get back onto the Trail of Medioc. It's the only way. Follow it until it splits in two then take the right fork until you come to the boulder - the gateway to the Festinol Kingdom.'

'But Badger!' Tom cried. 'He needs help. He's stranded at the edge of Bragenon. By now he could be dead.'

Moving forward, Lyal placed his hand gently on Tom's shoulder. 'Badger is safe,' he whispered. 'I found him a short while ago. That's when I knew you were in trouble.'

'Oh!' Tom gasped. 'But . . .' His words were suddenly drowned by a frenzy of fiendish howls.

'I can stay no longer,' Lyal said. 'You must hurry.'

'Lyal!' Tom shouted, remembering the wizard's shoe. 'I've lost . . . '

But the young man had vanished.

As the howling beasts drew closer, Tom raced along the trail like a hunted fox. When he reached the fork in the road he followed the path curving right, which took him through a narrow tract of leafy woodland. He sprinted along as fast as he could until he came to a huge, flat topped boulder, its smooth, slippery sides reaching almost as high as the top of his head. Pulling to a stop he stretched up onto his toes, his eyes scanning the surface of the stone. Then he saw it . . . a deep footprint chiselled into the edge.

At last he had reached the entrance to the Festinol Kingdom. But how was he going to get in without the wizard's shoe?

As the scream of approaching Grybb grew louder, panic began to play in his mind. Then he suddenly remembered Brignar leading him to the underground tunnels, and how he had moved the boulder by striking it three times with the sword. Quickly snatching the weapon from its scabbard, he raised it up. 'Please work,' he whispered, whacking the blade down with such force he was almost knocked off his feet. Once! Twice! Three times! Three loud clangs split the silence. Three resounding echoes rang through the air. But the boulder remained firmly in place. 'Nooooo,' he wailed.

By now he could hear the beasts racing along the trail. They were just at the other side of the trees. Squaring his back against the rock he rammed his heels into the earth, pushing so hard his body trembled and his face turned crimson. But no matter how hard he tried, the boulder would not budge. Then he saw the ferocious Grybb come tearing around the bend. He tried to scramble up the sides of the rock but it was

71

so worn and smooth, he kept slipping back down. They were almost upon him, ready to tear him limb from limb, when he spotted a small indent half way up the stone. Pushing his toe in, he launched himself up and just as one of the snarling brutes tried to grab hold of his foot, he landed on top of the boulder.

Springing to his feet he quickly drew the sword and when the largest of the beasts pounced, he swung the weapon down, instantly slicing its huge gargoyle head clean off its body. The rest of the pack momentarily froze, their astonished faces locked in shock. Then they slowly raised their heads, focused their bloodthirsty eyes on Tom and leapt at the rock like a pack of hungry lions.

He ran backwards and forwards, from one end to the other, trying to escape their snapping jaws. But suddenly, one of the beasts drew back and launching itself from the ground, landed right on top of the boulder. Tom leapt out of its way, his arms swaying like a see-saw as he tried to balance on the edge. As the snarling Grybb crept forward another grabbed the hem of his jacket. He felt himself toppling, falling towards its hungry jaws, when suddenly his foot slid across the stone, jamming tight into the chiselled out footprint.

An ear splitting crash ripped through the woodland sending the yelping Grybb scurrying for cover. Tom watched them retreat, his eyes glaring wide, when suddenly, he saw a split appear in the top of the rock. The next thing he knew, he was hurtling down a slippery wooden shaft, his sword still gripped tight in his hand. Landing with a thud on a huge bale of straw he swung his head around, fearful one of the beasts might have followed. But the boulder had snapped shut.

He blinked rapidly, trying to adjust his eyes to the dim light radiating from the rough stone walls. Then he saw them - a group of furry creatures resembling big fat, fluffy moles. They were small and round with huge brown eyes, chubby, oval faces and long, pointed noses. Most of them were dressed in simple tunics that stretched from their shoulders right down to their feet, but one of them, taller than the rest, wore an elaborate robe with a golden insignia embroidered across the front.

'I am Goodstad,' the creature smiled. 'King of the Festinol.' As he waddled forward his gaze slid uneasily along the length of Tom's sword. 'To encounter the death beasts and survive means you are brave indeed. Devole has chosen wisely. But,' he said, pointing to the shimmering blade. 'I would be grateful if you could put that away.'

'I thought I wasn't going to get in,' Tom gasped, ramming the sword into its scabbard as he climbed from the chute. 'I lost the wizard's shoe in the river.'

'Then it's fortunate your own shoe fitted the mould . . . very fortunate indeed. Now,' Goodstad smiled. 'I imagine you must be hungry.'

Tom hadn't thought about food for a long time, but the mention of it made him realise he hadn't eaten since he arrived. 'Starving!' he grinned.

Goodstad beckoned one of the others. 'Go prepare food for our guest. He will need sustenance before he can continue his journey.' Turning back to Tom he said. 'There is much to do and very little time to do it in. When you have eaten all you require, I will give you the second part of the map and provide you with all that is necessary to guide you on your way. Come . . . we must hurry.'

Tom followed the king to a vast underground cavern where hundreds of mole-like creatures were huddled together in

73

groups - the sound of their chattering voices buzzing around the rocky walls. As soon as Tom entered the chatter died away and gazing at him in silence, their eyes grew wide and wary. 'Forgive their curiosity,' Goodstad said. 'You are the first boy they have ever set eyes upon, and being unused to strangers, they are feeling a little nervous.'

Tom's attention was suddenly drawn to a pool situated at the very centre of the cavern. Its shimmering silver water, which looked as fluid as quicksilver and as glossy as a mirror, reflected hundreds of sparkling stalactites hanging from the high domed ceiling. At the edge of the pool, close to where Tom was standing, a rainbow coloured waterfall tumbled over clusters of luminous rocks, and where it entered the silver water, thousands of twinkling droplets, like microscopic stars, bounced from the surface.

'The Stinsal pool,' Goodstad said, 'one of the reasons for your passing through our kingdom. It will cleanse and refresh you, heal your wounds and give you the strength to continue your journey.'

Before he could say another word a loud yap echoed through the cavern, bouncing off the walls like a salvo of bullets. When Tom jerked around, he saw a little black dog bounding towards him.

'Badger!' he shrieked as the animal leapt into his outstretched arms, its tail beating furiously.

'He's missed you,' Goodstad chuckled. 'He was in a sorry state when Lyal brought him to us, but we managed to make him well again. Since then he's been agitated all the time, waiting very impatiently for you to arrive. It's been quite a task keeping him amused.'

74

'Thank you,' Tom said, his voice quivering with emotion as he gazed into Badger's eyes. 'I don't know what I would have done without him.'

'It's good to know he is safe,' Goodstad smiled. 'But for now . . . you must eat.'

The king led Tom to the edge of the Stinsal pool, where a small table had been filled with a strange concoction of food - black bread, pots of brightly coloured gooey stuff that looked like some kind of weird jam, blue and yellow cake drizzled with icing and a jug of peacock green, fizzy liquid with pink ice-cream floating on the top. When Tom sat down he was astounded by the wonderful aromas, better than anything he had ever smelled before. He spread a chunk of bread with a dollop of the gooey stuff, which tasted amazing, ate a slice of coloured cake, then washed it all down with the fizzy ice-cream drink.

'As we speak,' Goodstad said when Tom had finished eating, 'Arcos is summoning more horrors from Pendurak, to strengthen his protection of the Charquery Key. It is vital that you bathe in the Stinsal pool before you leave. Not only will it refresh you, it will help shield you from his magic.'

'The water looks a bit weird,' Tom said, staring at the silver liquid.

'Just wade in fully clothed,' Goodstad chuckled. 'When you emerge, you will be revitalised and better prepared for the dangers ahead.'

Tom made his way down a shallow incline until he reached the edge of the pool. Intrigued by the shimmering, silver liquid, he bent down and plunged his fingers in. It felt like water, it rippled like water, and better still, it was warm. He continued down the slope until the water reached his waist then he stopped. An exhilarating surge of energy suddenly swept through his aching limbs and as he watched the silver liquid lap over his arms, he saw the wounds on his wrists where the tethers had cut into his skin, miraculously heal. Inhaling a deep breath, he plunged beneath the surface, his eyes bursting wide when the silver water suddenly turned crystal clear. As the dirt leached from his clothes and the cuts and bruises covering his battered body rapidly disappeared, he dived to the bottom where an assortment of coloured stones winked and twinkled like jewels.

When he finally clambered from the water, refreshingly energised and miraculously dry, he saw Goodstad standing near the edge of the pool holding a piece of yellow parchment. 'This is the second part of the map,' he said.

Bending down he spread it over a large, flat rock, then pointed to an area marked in red. 'Here you leave the safety of our kingdom. You must continue along the trail of Medioc all the way to the Mountain of Delnar.' He slid his finger to the base of a mountain, where an ancient castle, protected by a high stone wall, stood shrouded in woodland. Then he pointed an ornate, iron gateway - at either side, stood an enormous bronze knight. 'In order to reach Delnar,' he said solemnly, 'you must pass through the grounds of Drogon's castle. We must prepare you well, for you will be in great danger.'

Fumbling in his pocket he pulled out a small silver flask and hurrying to the rainbow waterfall, filled it to the brim. 'As you can see,' he said, when he returned, 'the sentinels guarding the gates are armed with great killing swords. Their purpose is to prevent intruders. They will kill anyone who tries to pass between them. When you are close to the castle entrance, and before you are seen, drink half of this potion. The remainder you must keep for your return. It will make you and anything that touches you, invisible. Carry Badger in your arms and move quickly past the sentinels, but be sure to tread as quietly as a mouse, for the slightest sound will rouse them.

Sighing heavily, Goodstad lowered his eyes and staring at the ground said, 'Unfortunately, the forces of evil are growing stronger in our lands. Our defences are weakening. There was a time when we could calculate exactly how long our magic would last, now we have to rely more and more on presumption. It is impossible to say how long you will remain invisible, we can only hope the protection holds until you are safely out of danger. If you are captured, there is no telling what may become of you.'

Trying hard to suppress his increasing sense of unease, Tom frowned. 'Who is Drogon?' he asked. 'And why is no one allowed to enter his lands?'

Goodstad shook his head slowly from side to side and letting out a long, weary sigh, gazed sombrely into Tom's eyes. 'Drogon was my friend - a great knight of the noble Order of Zengal. Long ago he led his army into battle against an evil warlord named Grod. Though his forces were ultimately victorious, he was, for a time, held captive, and at the hands of his assailants, suffered horrific torture and mutilation. His disfigurement was so shocking that when he returned, he locked himself away, and unwilling to be looked upon, even by his friends, turned this castle into a fortress, forbidding anyone to enter. Rumour has it that his suffering and self imposed isolation has sent him mad. It is said that grotesque creatures stalk the castle grounds and should anyone manage to get past the sentinels guarding the gates, they will be eaten alive. Hence, since that time no one has ever tried to enter Drogon's domain. That is why it is vital you travel through his territory without being seen. Once you reach Delnar, you will be safe.'

Tom felt a shudder jolt down his spine but not wanting to let his fear be noticed, he took a deep breath, bit down hard on his lip and prayed the potion's magic would last.

'When you are safely through the gates, continue along the trail until you reach the wall at the other side of the castle.' Pointing to the map he said, 'If you push this stone here, the one I have marked with a cross, a concealed doorway will open. Proceed up the mountain until you reach a waterfall, behind which lies a tunnel. Before you enter the tunnel it is vital that you arm yourself with protection. The inside of the mountain is hotter than anyone can bear and to gain immunity from the heat, you must inhale the perfume of the Stellusaris flower. You will find it growing around the edges of the waterfall and will recognise it by the colour and shape of its flowers, which are striped with gold and silver and resemble tiny birds in flight.'

Fiddling in his pocket, Goodstad removed a bronze medallion. Dangling it in front of Tom's eyes, he said, 'This is the seal of the eastern wizard, which will gain you entry into Delnar. At the end of the tunnel lies an enormous crater with a burning rock standing at its centre. When you place the seal upon the firerock, Zafror will be alerted to your presence. But you must hurry, for somewhere in the mountain sleeps an enormous Gavad Spineclaw - the biggest and most aggressive of the dragons. His name is Traak. He has two fire breathing heads, scales as thick as armour plate and is said to be as big as the mountain itself. Should he awake, you must show him the medallion - only then will he allow you to pass in safety. Moving towards Tom, he slid the chain gently over the boy's head. 'Protect this seal with your life. And be sure to keep it safely out of sight.'

Tom lifted the medallion until it was just a few inches from his eyes, carefully examining the strange symbols engraved around its edge, then, to be sure it could not be seen he pushed it down the neck of his shirt.

'The time has come for you to leave,' Goodstad said, trying to disguise the note of concern in his voice. 'Come, follow me.' He led Tom through a doorway in the cavern wall, then along a narrow passageway until they reached a set of wooden stairs. 'The trapdoor above,' he said, pointing upwards, 'brings you out onto the Trail of Medioc. You will be close to the Mountain of Delnar and far enough away from where you entered our kingdom to ensure the Grybb have lost your scent.' When he handed Tom the second part of the map, and saw him push it down the side of his sock, he smiled.

'The wizard's map's down the other one!' Tom grinned'

Pulling a lever at the side of the stairway, Goodstad released the trapdoor. 'When you come out onto the surface turn to your right then follow the trail until you reach the castle grounds. The forest will provide you with cover, but stay well out of sight as you approach the gates and be sure to drink the Stinsal water before you are seen. Do not move into the open until you are completely invisible.' Placing his hand on Tom's shoulder, he squeezed it tight. 'Good luck my friend.'

Tom lifted Badger into his arms and made his way to the top of the stairs. Poking his head through the trapdoor, his eyes just above ground level, he cautiously looked around. The Grybb were nowhere to be seen. When satisfied it was safe to proceed he quickly scrambled out. Then he watched the trapdoor slide quietly to a close, leaving no visible sign of its existence.

CHAPTER 7

Tom was standing in a shady woodland grove, where a heavy scent of blossom filled the air and birds twittered high in the treetops. Placing Badger on the ground, he turned to his right and creeping warily from one tree to the next, made his way to the edge of the thicket. Drawing to a halt behind an enormous oak, he paused for a second just to be sure it was safe. Then he peered cautiously around the trunk. He saw the Trail of Medioc snake across a strip of stony ground then disappear into a swathe of dense forest. Raising his eyes, he glimpsed the turrets and towers of Drogon's castle rising through the treetops like silent, fossilised giants. 'Come on Badger,' he shuddered. 'Let's go.'

They moved along with slow, steady steps, all the while watching and listening for any sign of the Grybb. Coming into the open they quickened their pace - a nervous flutter dancing in the pit of Tom's stomach as he heard his footsteps crunching along the gravel track. When they entered the woodland it looked dark and gloomy, the trees huddled so close their branches blocked out most of the light - but Tom didn't mind, he felt safer with the cover of the forest. With Badger trotting by his side, he sprinted along the trail until he came close to the castle wall. Through the few remaining trees, he could see huge slabs of stone rising from the ground. At this point the trail veered off to the right, far enough into the woodland to keep him from being seen.

Lifting Badger into his arms he ducked down low and creeping steadily forward followed the path through the trees. When he reached a spot where he could see the entrance to the castle grounds he stopped. The gates were standing open and just as the map had shown, two gigantic bronze knights, as tall and as broad as windmills, were standing guard. They were motionless, and as if unmoved for decades their sightless eyes stared out across the landscape.

Careful not to make a sound, Tom tucked Badger under his arm then pulled the small silver flask from his pocket. He slowly eased out the stopper, gasping as the pungent odour caught his breath. With his fingers shaking he raised the bottle to his lips, gulped down half the liquid then pushed it back into his pocket. Suddenly, a wave of dizziness swept from his head to his feet. Then his body, shimmering like an image on water, completely disappeared. Raising his hands, he slid them slowly across his face, then, feeling the gentle tap, tap, tap of Badger's heart beating against his arm, he looked down. All he could see was the forest floor. He walked around in a circle and unable to see his feet, stamped the ground in order to confirm that he was still there. But then, suddenly realising the noise might give him away he jerked to a stop. Holding his breath, he stood absolutely still, listening for the slightest sound. But the woodland remained silent.

Tiptoeing forward he crept cautiously through the trees, and when the sentinels came fully into view, their huge broadswords crossed in front of the open gates, he stopped. He smiled when he saw how easy it would be to slip between them. Concentrating hard on the sound of his footsteps he pushed past a tangle of leafy branches and moved out into the open. But he failed to notice the loud swish as the branches sprang back into place.

A flash of sunlight speared from one of the sentinel's swords. The blade was rising slowly from the ground. As a deafening screech crashed through the silence one of the knights turned its head, its lifeless eyes, locked into oblivion only moments before, now peering into the woodland. Suddenly the warrior tore its huge metal feet from the earth and in two enormous strides, crashed them down right in front of Tom. It leaned forward, moving its head slowly from side to side and as he froze with fear, its cold, blank eyes fixed on the very spot where he was standing.

At that moment another deafening screech rang out - the other bronze warrior was thundering towards them. Knowing he could soon be splattered like a trampled beetle Tom leapt out of its way and raced towards the gate, the boom of clanging footsteps covering the sound of his own. In just a few desperate strides he was through, sprinting for the cover of a nearby tree.

Peering around the trunk he watched the bronze knights stomp backwards and forwards, searching for the source of the disturbance. After a while they drew to a shuddering halt and turning full circle, examined the woods, the castle wall and finally, the castle grounds. Then they suddenly thundered forward, their huge metal feet booming across the earth. Thinking they had seen him Tom darted out of sight, his body tense with fear, his heart pounding like a drum. But when the sentinels reached the gates they thudded to a stop and resuming their positions, one at either side, took a final look around then swung their huge broadswords down across the entrance. Within moments they looked as if they had never moved.

'Phew!' Tom gasped, still shaking like a leaf, 'that was close. Come on Badger, let's get out of here.' To be certain his footsteps could not be heard, he kept off the path and trotted along the grass at the edge of the trail.

Eventually, after moving safely past the castle, he came to the bottom of a steep incline. Looking up, he saw the trail disappear into darkness through a huddle of leafy trees. Time to check the map, he thought.

After carefully examining the area to make sure it was safe, he knelt on the ground and eased the parchment from his sock. Knowing it would remain invisible for as long as he was touching it, he spread it on the ground then wedged a stone at each of its corners. When he let go, the map came fully into view.

Starting at the castle gates, he slid his gaze across the map until he came to the spot where the ground sloped upwards. At the top of the incline, behind a row of leafy trees, stood the castle wall, and on the other side of the wall, in big letters, were the words 'Mountain of Delnar'. At last, Tom thought, feeling a sudden twinge of optimism. We're almost there.

Quickly removing the corner stones, he refolded the map and pushed it down the side of his sock. Then his eyes burst wide with alarm. He could see his fingers - they were quivering like a mirage. Looking down he saw Badger taking shape in his arms, and shuddering with horror, watched helplessly as his legs and feet become visible. 'No,' he whispered.

Suddenly vulnerable he ducked down low and wrenched the small silver flask from his pocket. He stared at it uncertainly - desperately wanting to drink the rest of the liquid - desperately wanting to stay invisible. But if he did, there would be none left for his return. Terrified, he peered along the trail, his gaze moving to the top of the incline . . . the mountain was just behind those trees, if he hurried he would soon be out of the castle grounds and safe.

Putting Badger down, he shoved the bottle back into his pocket and leaping to his feet, started running up the slope.

But as the little dog raced ahead, Tom noticed a stringent smell. Looking up he saw a thin, white mist swirling close to the ground. 'Come back!' he called. When Badger turned, his body went limp and he slumped to the floor. Tom shot towards him but as he scooped the little dog into his arms, he felt a wave of dizziness sweep through him. He staggered forward, trying to reach the top of the slope, but his legs suddenly gave way and he thudded to the ground. Gasping for breath he heard a noise coming from somewhere below. Then his mind went black and he lost consciousness.

At the bottom of the incline, two fat, foul smelling creatures waddled from the trees. They wore stained leather jerkins and scruffy, torn pants that scraped the ground as they shuffled along. 'Do yer think they're dead?' the smaller one asked as its snout twitched and its mouth drooled saliva.

'How do I know? Let's 'av a look.'

They shuffled up the slope huffing and puffing, their little beady eyes darting all around. When they reached the spot where Tom was sprawled on the ground unconscious, they staggered to a halt. The larger creature was holding a thick, knobbly stick and as Tom twitched and groaned, he poked it hard into his ribs. This caused Tom to kick his leg out sending his assailant reeling backwards, crashing hard into his companion.

'Ouch! Stingle. Ouch!'

'Quiet!' Stingle grunted. 'Go get the cage before 'e wakes up . . . before we're seen.'

'Always givin' orders,' the smaller creature grumbled as he waddled down the slope. 'Can't do anythin' 'imself.'

After disappearing into the woods, he soon emerged pulling a rickety wooden cage mounted on two creaking wheels. Positioning it at the bottom of the incline he shuffled back to Stingle, who was holding Tom's feet, trying to drag him down. 'Quick, Pover,' he grunted. 'You grab one foot, I'll get the other.'

Bumping and bashing into one another, they dragged Tom to the bottom of the slope and heaving him inside the cage, hastily tied his wrists to the wooden bars.

'Now, Pover, go an' get the other one.'

'Nah . . . not worth it . . . too small.'

'Bring 'im you idiot!' Stingle snarled, clouting Pover around the ear. 'Or 'e'll be seen.'

'Ouch! Oh yeah! Sorry Stingle . . . wasn't thinkin'.' As he waddled up the slope, holding his painful ear, he muttered something under his breath. Moments later he shuffled back down with Badger slung over his shoulder. Throwing the little dog into the back of the cage, he secured the door then glanced warily about. 'Come on Stingle, let's get movin', before someone sees us.'

Turning into the woods they threaded their way down a narrow mud track, all the while quarrelling and poking at each other. Every time the cart wheels got stuck in the earth, Stingle, who was the biggest and nastiest of the two, clouted Pover with a stick

'I'm sick of this,' Pover finally grunted. 'Sick of you blaming me fer everythin'. In fact, I don't even want to be yer brother no more.' Letting out a long, heavy groan he wiped the sweat from his bristled face, let go of the cart and waddled to a nearby tree. 'I'm stayin' 'ere,' he moaned,

85

slumping wearily to the ground. 'If yer think yer so cleaver, then do it yerself.'

'Get up!' Stingle snarled, jerking the cart to a standstill. 'We've got to get back. You know what'll 'appen if we're caught?' He strode towards the tree and was about to jab Pover in the belly, when something made him stop. Turning his head, he squeezed his black, beady eyes to slits. Then he let out a long, gasping wail. 'Stupid!' he growled, 'why didn't you take it?'

'Take what?'

Hurtling back to the cage, he stuck his arm through the bars and stretching as far as his fat belly would allow, slid his thick, warty fingers towards the hilt of Tom's sword. But he couldn't quite reach it.

'You should've took it!' he groaned. Grabbing a stone from the ground, he flung it at Pover's head. 'You should've took the sword.'

'Ouch! Oh! Ouch!' Pover squealed, scurrying back to the cage. 'What sword?'

'That sword you idiot!'

'What'll we do now Stingle? He'll kill us. What'll we do?'

'Stop bleatin', I'll sort it out later. Just grab the 'andle an' get a move on. If we don't get back we'll be caught.'

The first thing Tom noticed as he edged back to consciousness was a heavy scent of woodland mingled with the groan of creaking wood. He could feel his body swaying from side to side and when he opened his eyes, blinking to clear the blur from his vision, he realised he was sitting in a rickety wooden cage. Badger was lying close to his feet - his body still, his breathing shallow. Above the rattle of the cartwheels he could hear a jabber of voices and peering through the bars, saw two hog like creatures puffing and panting as they hauled the cage through the woods. Where were they taking him? What were they going to do with him?

Jerking his wrists, he tried to free his arms, but every time he tugged he felt the tethers tighten against his skin. Determined to break free he kept on trying until finally, when the thongs cut into his wrists, he let out a loud shriek of pain.

The cart suddenly jerked to a halt.

When the two scruffy creatures came hurtling towards it, Tom got a whiff of their revolting stench and trying to hold his breath, he felt his stomach turn.

Almost crashing into the bars, jostling to be first, Stingle grabbed Pover's arm and hauled him out of the way. Barely glancing at Tom he waddled to the rear of the cage, his wet snout twitching wildly. When he saw the wound in Tom's wrist and the thin line of blood trickling down the wooden bars, his eyes darted fearfully from side to side. Carefully examining the woodland, he made a succession of short, nervous grunts then stuck a fat, warty finger into the blood, shoved it into his mouth and sucked it clean. 'Mmm,' he drooled as his tongue lashed over his brown stained tusks. 'Tasty morsel this is? Come on Pover, let's get out of 'ere before we're seen . . . and 'urry . . . I'm starvin'.'

The cage was brought to rest at the edge of a wide forest clearing, where discarded animal bones littered the ground and a rotten smell permeated the air. A ramshackle array of shabby wooden huts ran around the edge of the clearing, their window openings stuffed with muddles of broken twigs, their doorways covered with lengths of filthy sacking. At the front of each hut a group of hog-like creatures lay sleeping - their fat bodies breathing in and out to the rhythm of their grunting snores.

Hearing the creak of the cart, one of them opened its eyes and turning its head in the direction of the sound, saw what looked like two shadowy figures approaching. Thinking, in its half awakened state that the camp was under attack, it started squealing like a startled pig. The others leapt to their feet and crashing around in terror quickly scurried for the safety of the dilapidated shelters.

'It's Stingle you idiots! An' I've fetched yer somethin'. Yer'll soon be eatin' a nice roast dinner.' Dozens of beady eyes peered from the twiggy covered windows and moments later, as the ragged door coverings were ripped aside, several scruffy creatures waddled into the open. Though they were extremely short sighted, unable to see anything clearly if it was more than a few strides away, their twitching snouts confirmed their leader's presence.

'Look what I've got,' Stingle grinned, beckoning them towards the cart. 'Don't say I never gets yer nothin'.' When they saw Tom and Badger they squeaked and squealed with excitement, their greedy eyes glowing with approval.

The stink of their sweaty bodies made Tom's stomach retch and angered by their leering glares, he started bouncing up and down, making the cage creak and shake. 'Get lost! You stink!' he bellowed. 'Get away from me!' His voice was so wild and angry it sent the startled creatures racing around in a fit of panic, colliding so hard into each other they all fell flat on their faces.

Chuckling at their stupidity, Stingle waddled towards Pover, who was leaning on a tree at the edge of the clearing watching the commotion. 'Get that crazy lot buildin' a fire,' he grunted, 'but keep four of 'em standing guard by the cage. I don't want 'im escapin'.' Turning, he shuffled away in the direction of the huts.

'Oi!' Pover shouted, as the terrified creatures scrambled to their feet. 'Come 'ere, I've got somethin' for yer to do.' Scurrying towards him, glad to be as far away from Tom as they could get, they closed together in a circle, listening intently to what he had to say. He hadn't been speaking for long when a cheer suddenly exploded from the group, then, grunting excitedly they all disappeared into the forest. Soon they were trundling from the trees carrying armfuls of sticks and brushwood, a process they repeated over and over again until a huge bonfire had been created.

The three chosen to stand guard, demonstrated their disagreement with a barrage of squeals and foot thudding, but when told that they would not take part in the feast if they didn't obey, they fell into sulky silence. Conceding defeat, they begrudgingly shuffled behind Pover as he made his way to the cage. When Tom saw them approaching he decided to amuse himself by creating as much discomfort for them as he could. After all, it would help keep the fear of what they were planning to do to him at bay.

As they settled nervously into position, two at either side, Pover gave them a condescending grin then waddled away. Their eyes kept darting to Tom every few seconds and when he started thudding his feet on the floor and screeching like a trapped pig, they trembled with fear. He spat and screamed and shrieked and made so much noise that they were soon clinging to each other like demented monkeys. He could hardly believe how easy they were to scare.

89

After a while, Stingle appeared from one of the dismal hovels and lumbering towards the centre of the clearing shouted, 'Get that fire goin', an' be quick about it!' Turning slowly, he waddled towards the cage. 'What's all the commotion about?' he grunted.

'What'll we do Stingle?' one of the terrified creatures squealed. 'E's mad. 'E'll kill us if we try to get 'im out.'

''E'll kill us all,' the others chorused.

Licking the moisture from his snout, Stingle fumbled inside his jerkin and pulling out a long, thin chord, just like the one binding Tom's wrists, he held it up for all to see. 'This'll sort 'im out,' he grinned. When he placed the thong onto his hand it slithered across his palm then coiled around his fat, stubby fingers. 'One of these round 'is throat an' should 'e move so much as an inch, 'ell be a goner! Heh, heh, heh.'

There was a spiteful glint in the foul smelling creature's eye as he trundled along the side of the cage. Pausing, he pushed his hand through the bars and dangling the wriggling thong in front of Tom's face, slavered with delight. Then he shuffled on, and when he disappeared around the back, Tom felt something cold slither around his neck then tighten against his skin.

'Now!' Stingle grunted, moving back into Tom's line of sight, 'That should keep yer quiet!' Licking saliva from his dripping snout, he waddled away. 'Get that fire goin.' he roared. 'I'm starvin' ungry.'

When Pover ambled up to the three creatures standing guard - the ones Tom had been terrifying only moments before - he saw they were now almost purring with delight. 'Time to get yer own back,' he sniggered, pointing to a stack of twigs at the edge of the trees. The creatures scurried away and when they returned, each armed with a long, pointed stick, they ran around screaming with excitement. Then, drawing close together, their beady eyes resting on Tom, they shuffled towards the cage and started jabbing at his flesh.

'Yer not so scary now!' Pover grunted, as one of the creatures rammed its stick so hard into Tom's ankle it punctured his flesh. When the others saw a glint of shiny blood bubble to the surface, they each took a turn at jabbing and stabbing, until his leg was covered with masses of bleeding wounds.

'Not so scary now!' they all chorused

Stingle, who was at the centre of the compound helping to ignite the bonfire, suddenly spun around. Staring in the direction of the cage he squeezed his eyes to slits. Seeing only a smudge of blurred images, he raised his snout and sniffed the air. Then he suddenly slung the lighted torch to the ground and charged across the clearing.

'Get yer thievin' mitts off,' he roared, shoving Pover and the others out of the way. ''E's mine!'

As the terrified creatures scattered in all directions, trying to get as far away from their furious leader as they could, Stingle's black, beady eyes settled on the bloody tracks running down Tom's legs. He sniffed and slavered, pressed his face up to the bars, glaring at the pools of blood collecting on the floor. 'Can't resist a little taste,' he grunted, sliding his chubby fingers towards them.

'Arghh!' Tom yelled, stamping hard on the creature's hand. 'Get away!'

Jerking back, screaming in agony, Stingle shoved his throbbing fingers into his mouth and rocking backwards and forwards, started squealing like a baby. When Pover and the others heard his desperate cries they came hurtling back to the cage, but seeing the infantile display of pain demonstrated by their leader, they bent their heads to hide their smirking faces.

'Get the spit in place,' Stingle suddenly roared, almost exploding with rage. 'We're gonna roast 'im alive'. Turning to Tom he sneered callously. 'In case you're wonderin' who we are. We are the Scaggy. An' we'll soon be eating you up for dinner.' With that he waddled away.

CHAPTER 8

The thong Stingle had placed around Tom's throat was now squeezing so tight he hardly dared move, and when a tangy cloud of wood smoke wafted into his lungs, he tried hard not to cough in case it coiled even tighter.

Hearing the crackle of burning wood he slid his eyes slowly in the direction of the sound, and careful not to move a muscle, saw the Scaggy dragging a huge iron spit towards the blazing bonfire. As he watched them heave the clumsy piece of metal into place, huffing and puffing, swearing and cursing, he heard a scratching noise - it was coming from the floor of the cage. Sliding his eyes back slowly, he saw Badger scrambling to his feet.

A flood of relief surged through him as he watched the little dog shake vigorously then gaze around as if trying to figure out where he was. It wasn't long before Badger started stumbling around the cage, his tail tucked between his legs, his eyes trying hard to focus, and though it took several moments for his vision to clear, he eventually saw Tom slumped against the bars. Making a low whimpering sound he wobbled towards him and crawled onto his lap. Puzzled by the absence of stroking hands he stretched up and rested his paws on Tom's shoulders . . . then he started to lick his face.

'No!' Tom whispered, careful not to move his lips. But that was all it took to make the thongs pull tighter - they were soon squeezing so hard that his face turned blue and he was gasping for breath. 'Help,' he tried to cry, but the sound that escaped his mouth was no more that a weak gush of air. At that moment a cloudy, black haze engulfed him.

By now Badger's ears were pricked and his nose twitching rapidly - he could smell something strange. Staring into Tom's bulging eyes he tilted his head, first to one side, then to the other. Then his gaze fixed on the thong fastened tight around Tom's neck. Like a bolt of lightening he suddenly lunged forward, grasped it between his needle sharp teeth and with one swift tug, ripped it away. Flinging it to the floor, he leapt from Tom's knee and tore it to shreds.

As a rush of air flooded his lungs, Tom's eyes burst open. 'Badger,' he wheezed, coughing and spluttering, 'you're terrific. But I need you to do one more thing . . . I want you to free my hands before those idiots come back. Quick! Behind me!'

Badger squeezed between Tom and the cage bars, emerging moments later with a wriggling thong hanging from the sides of his mouth. Growling viciously, he bit it in two then slung it to the floor.

'Come on,' Tom whispered, let's get out of here. But as he crept towards the door he heard a jabber of excited voices approaching. Signalling Badger to lie down he darted back to the bars, grabbed the pieces of lifeless thong from the floor and wrapped them around his neck. Sliding back into position, he pushed his hands behind his back.

'I'm not goin' in!' Pover squealed, his feet thudding to a resolute stop as he reached the cage door.

'Me neither!' another grunted

'Then who's goin' t'get 'im out?'

'I don't care,' Pover shouted, 'so long as it ain't me!'

94

'You know very well who's goin' to get 'im out!' A sudden commotion of squeaks and squeals erupted from the group as Stingle bulldozed his way to the front. 'That's why I'm leader! Cos I'm braver than all of you lot put together!' Squeezing his little beady eyes to slits he peered through the door slats. 'Just be sure,' he grunted, fumbling with the rickety lock. 'When we shares 'em out, I gets the 'eds. The 'eds is mine.'

There was an eerie creak as the door swung open. Squashing his fat body through the narrow gap, Stingle grunted, then paused. He peered around the cage, his wet snout twitching, his eyes darting from one side to the other. Then, as his gaze fell on the fuzzy shape lying motionless by his feet, he gave it a hefty kick and shuffled on.

Tom was slumped against the bars, his eyes closed and his head flopped to one side. Making a succession of nervous squeals, Stingle glared at him for several moments. Then he noticed a thin line of sweat trickling down the side of the boy's face. He sniffed and grunted, and moving closer, prodded a wary finger into his chest. Tom did not move. Deciding he must be asleep, unconscious or dead, Stingle leaned down closer. 'Let's get yer on the fire,' he muttered, reaching towards the thong. But when he ripped it from Tom's throat, he suddenly jerked back. The thong wasn't moving. Letting out a sudden squeal of terror he swung around. But Badger was blocking his path, snarling like a rabid hyena.

'Move any further and I'll slice your head off,' Tom growled, digging the tip of his sword into the terrified creature's back.

'Don't kill me. Please don't kill me.' Stingle pleaded. 'I'll do anythin'. Just don't kill me.'

'Then get over there and don't move!'

'Yes sir. I'll do anythin' sir. Anythin'.'

When Tom and Badger leapt from the cage, the terrified Scaggy scattered in panic. 'Go get them Badger!' Tom yelled.

After securing the rusty lock he sprinted to the bonfire then tossed the key into the roaring flames, while Badger raced towards the woodland, cutting three of the fleeting creatures off. Nipping at their heels like a dog herding sheep, he drove them back to the centre of the clearing, where Tom was standing by the crackling fire swinging his gleaming sword.

'How about roasting you?' he roared, grabbing a burning stick from the flames and wafting it under their noses.

'No! No! Please!' they shrieked.

'If you want to stay alive take me back to where you found me. And hurry!'

'Yes sir.' Pover squealed. 'Anythin' you want sir, anythin'.'

'No tricks,' Tom growled. 'Or I'll chop off your heads!'

'No sir! We promise sir! It's just over there . . . but . . . '

'No buts. Just do it,' Tom yelled.

As they moved further and further away from the camp, Tom noticed that the Scaggy were becoming increasingly anxious. They waddled through the trees clasping each others hands, their frightened eyes darting everywhere. When they reached the edge of a wide forest clearing, where dazzling sunlight flooded the ground, they pulled to a sudden halt, and seemingly terrified of moving into the open, refused to go any further.

'If you want to keep your heads, get going,' Tom yelled, prodding each of them in the back with the tip of his sword.

Though they were reluctant to move, he managed to force them forward a few nervous steps at a time. Progress was extremely slow and when they reached the centre of the clearing they stopped dead. Their eyes scanned the forest, their wet snouts twitched as they cautiously sniffed the air. Then leaping up and down, squealing in panic, they pointed to the edge of the woodland. Squinting through the blinding glare, Tom saw a cluster of distorted shapes wavering beneath the trees. Unable to make out what they were, he shielded his eyes from the sun. Then a jolt of fear shot through him. A company of mounted soldiers were blocking the way.

Suddenly the Scaggy started running towards the horsemen. 'He's forcin' us to lead 'im to the castle.' Pover screamed when they finally jerked to a halt' He's come to kill Drogon!'

An ominous silence descended, broken only by the thud of agitated hooves pounding the forest floor. Then a gigantic warrior, his scarlet cloak falling starkly against the sheen of his polished armour, leaned forward in his saddle. 'Scaggy,' he breathed.

The minute he thrust a clenched first into the air, the army spread out, forming a wide circle around the edge of the clearing. Then four horsemen rode forward, heading straight for the startled Scaggy. Screaming with terror the creatures swung around and darting about in a flurry of panic, tried desperately to find an escape. But the soldiers took chase and one by one ran the squealing creatures to the ground. Obeying a gesture of command from their leader, they drew their swords and lopped each of the Scaggys' heads clean off.

Alone at the centre of the clearing, Tom gasped in horror. When he saw the horsemen turn, his legs began to tremble. With fear pulsing through his veins he thrust out his sword and as they charged straight towards him, sweeping their blades within inches of his body, he ducked and dived, dodged and sidestepped. But the soldiers swung around, charging at him over and over again until he was so weak and confused, he could barely lift his sword. Crushed and defeated he slumped to the ground, his weapon slipping lightly from his fingers. As he lay there panting, his heart hammering in his chest, he heard the thud of approaching hooves. They stopped close to where he lay. Knowing he was about to be exterminated he reached for his sword, but as his trembling fingers closed around the hilt, a booted foot clamped it to the ground.

'So! You come to kill Drogon?' an angry voice growled.

As Tom raised his head, blinking his weary eyes, he saw the scarlet cloaked warrior looming over him like an angry bear, his metal helmet glinting in the sunlight. 'The Scaggy lied,' he gasped. 'I don't want to kill anyone. I just want to get out of here.'

'Get out?' the warrior roared, 'No one gets out of here.' Lifting Tom's sword from the ground he climbed back onto his horse. 'Bring him to the castle.' he bellowed.

Tom's arms were forced behind his back then tied together at the wrists. Flanked by two heavily armoured horsemen he was led to the rear of the regiment, which had formed two orderly lines behind their leader. They travelled through an area of dense woodland then moved up a winding slope towards an austere looking castle. The gatehouse, which was protected by an impenetrable portcullis, stood between two immense stone towers, beyond which lay a wide expanse of cobbled courtyard.

When they reached the top of the incline, the scarlet cloaked warrior signalled his army to halt. At that moment his gleaming black stallion started prancing and whinnying, beating its hooves impatiently on the heavily gravelled track. Then, as the gateway rumbled open, groaning like an enormous metal demon, it bolted through so fast, its hooves sent a shower of sparks flickering off the cobbles.

When the rest of the army were safely inside, the portcullis shuddered to a close, and as the soldiers climbed from their saddles, dozens of spindly limbed creatures with pallid skin and bony features, hurried into the courtyard, their upturned noses twitching incessantly. Each of the strange creatures took charge of a horse and as they moved away, one behind the other in meticulous precision, Tom noticed a mark imprinted into the backs of each of their heads. His gaze followed them until they disappeared through a huge door set into the castle wall.

Hearing footsteps he swung around. The scarlet cloaked warrior was striding towards him, his crimson cloak swirling around his feet, his helmet tucked under one arm. When he drew to a halt, Tom saw a ragged purple scar running across his cheekbone and the remnant of a partially severed ear hanging beneath a main of unruly, black hair. There was fury on his stern, frowning face, suspicion in his dark, accusing eyes.

'I am Valtok!' he boomed, exuding the power of an agitated bull. 'Commander of the mighty Zengal army.' Raising Tom's sword, he cast a cursory glance over the gleaming blade. 'So!' he roared. 'You bring a powerful weapon to perform your evil deed.' He glared at Tom for several moments, his eyes conveying the hatred he felt inside. Then, swinging around, he signalled two of the soldiers. 'Take him to the dungeons. Like the filthy Scaggy, he will die!'

Tom was escorted into the castle by two armed guards, who led him through a thick, wooden door fortified with strips of metal and heavy iron studs. When the bolt was rammed into place behind him, a chilling echo resonated through a labyrinth of corridors, sending a chill shuddering down his spine. They descended a flight of dismal, stone steps then moved through a network of dimly lit passageways until they came to a circular dungeon. Tom was hauled inside and marched to the centre, where a leg-iron, attached to the floor by a thick metal chain, was fastened around his ankle.

'What will happen to me?' he asked, as the ropes binding his wrists were cut free.

'The master will decide.'

'How long will I be kept here?'

'Until the master decides.'

When the guards withdrew, he could hear their footsteps moving further and further away, and as they trailed into the distance, he felt the chill of isolation sweep through him. He gazed around the sparse contents of his prison, his eyes coming to rest on a few bales of straw and a large candle positioned at the edge of the floor. Apart from that, the dungeon was empty - its cold, grey walls towering high above him. He moved his eyes upwards, from one huge slab of stone to the next. When they reached the top of the wall, he saw sunlight streaming through a wide opening circling the top of the tower . . . if only he could reach it.

He tugged at the heavy leg chain, jerking his leg and heaving every time it clanked against the rough, uneven flags. But there was no way he was going to break it, no way he was going to escape. Sliding wearily to the ground he rested his elbows on his knees and placed his head between his hands. Then his thoughts slowly drifted away, back to the last time he had seen his little dog. It was in the clearing, just before the soldiers killed the Scaggy. Had they killed Badger too?

Lost in a wave of emotion, he failed to notice a noise coming from the other side of a small doorway in the dungeon wall - a kind of dull rasping sound - like a rusty bolt being drawn back. After a pause, the door gave a whining creak then eased open, another creak, it opened a little more. Then, after a moment's hesitation, one of the spindly limbed creatures Tom had seen in the courtyard crept through, its huge hooded eyes darting nervously from side to side.

'Quick!' the creature whispered. 'Lock the door behind me. If he escapes, we're for it.' As it edged around the curve of the wall, its thin, gangly body pressed against the stone, its nose twitched incessantly.

'Who are you?' Tom mumbled, raising his head.

The creature stopped, its eyes glaring wide. 'My name is Fergil. I have come to light the candle and give you straw for comfort.' Scurrying across the floor, it drew a thin, metal rod from its pocket and when it touched the candle wick, a vibrant flame flickered into life. 'May I . . . er . . . may I ask your name?' it said, its eyes darting constantly between Tom and the door.

101

'My name is Tom . . . Thomas Goodwin.'

'Do you come to kill the master as they say?'

'No!' Tom shouted angrily. 'The Scaggy lied. I need to get out of here.'

'My master, Drogon, forbids anyone to enter his lands. As you have broken his command, you must remain here until he decides your fate.' Trembling slightly, the timid creature edged forward. 'Tell me,' it whispered. 'If you did not come to kill the master, why are you here . . . and how did you manage to get past the sentinels guarding the gate?'

'Stop asking questions!' Tom shouted. 'I've told you, I did not come to kill Drogon. I just need to get out of here. I must!' When he suddenly sprang to his feet, the timid creature leapt across the flagstones so fast it went sprawling across the floor. 'Who is this Drogon anyway?' Tom yelled. 'Who sends his soldiers to hunt and kill? He must be an evil toad!'

'No. No.' Fergil groaned, rubbing the lump that was forming on his forehead as he scrambled to his feet. 'There is much misunderstanding. Please. My master is a good man. If I tell you about him . . . if I explain all he has been through . . . the agony he has endured, maybe you will understand. Maybe then you will be able to tell me where you are going and why you are here.'

'Explain all you like.' Tom said, slumping to the floor. 'But I will tell you nothing.'

Edging back to the candle, Fergil settled on the flagstones beneath its flickering light. 'To explain my master's plight,' he began, his downcast eyes filling with tears, 'I must go back to the time when an evil warlord plotted to conquer

102

Keeros and spread chaos throughout the land. The warlord's name was Grod.'

Tom remembered Goodstad telling him of a battle between Drogon and an evil warlord, but not wanting to give the creature any clue as to why he was there, he remained silent.

'The warlord lived in the Blacklands, a twilight zone separated from the rest of Keeros by an invisible barrier through which no living thing can pass. His lifelong ambition was to obliterate the Keepers of order and take control of our lands. To achieve it he enlisted the help of the Dark Warrior Kings, wicked sorcerers who thrive on chaos and destruction. Long ago, they had been banished to an area of the Blacklands known as the region of shadows, a dismal place filled with gloom and desolation, and as long as The Keepers ruled Keeros, they were unable to return. They provided the warlord with a way of passing through the invisible barrier and gave him gold enough to equip a mighty army. Then, as an extra measure of protection, they bestowed upon him the gift of immortality. From that moment on, Grod could never be slain.'

'To build his army, he enlisted thousands of Gnomags, evil creatures devoid of emotion, who murder and maim to get what they desire . . . and more than anything else in life, they desire power. Entering Keeros from the north, the warlord slaughtered entire communities, burnt dwellings and laid claim to vast territories. Those not massacred were captured and enslaved.' Turning his head, Fergil pointed to the brand burned deep into the base of his skull. 'As you can see, many of us were forced into slavery.'

'When the onslaught began, Keeros had little by way of defences. Peace and harmony had reigned for thousands of years and the noble Order of Zengal, once a proud and

103

mighty army dedicated to the protection of our lands, had almost died out. There were however, two brothers remaining - Drogon and Valtok. Being descendants of Zengal they possessed a special gift, which, long ago had been bestowed on every member of the order. They had the power to reverse the magic of the Dark Warrior Kings. Grod could indeed be slain, but only by a true descendant of the noble order.'

'When Grod launched his attack, Drogon and Valtok were summoned to the highest court in the land. Ordered to recruit an army to crush the invading forces, Drogon, the eldest, was appointed leader, with Valtok, his brother, second in command.'

'Thousands of men, whose homes and families had been cruelly destroyed, were eager to enlist. Driven by an overwhelming desire to seek retribution they came from far and wide, from every corner of Keeros, and as the army moved from village to village in pursuit of the warlord, hundreds more joined their cause. Soon Grod's forces were outnumbered two to one, and when confronted in battle, the evil Gnomags were swiftly wiped out, leaving their leader crushed and beaten.'

'With no more than a handful of soldiers, the warlord made his escape, but knowing Drogon and Valtok would pursue him, he set a trap with the help of a cowardly band of creatures known as Scaggy.'

'Scaggy!' Tom exclaimed. 'It was the Scaggy who captured me in the forest. They were mercilessly slaughtered by Valtok's soldiers. It was awful.'

'Yes,' Fergil said, gazing sadly into Tom's eyes. 'But Valtok's hatred for these vile creatures is well founded. In exchange for gold, the Scaggy agreed to set a trap - one which would deliver the Zengal leaders into the warlord's hands. They posted look outs at strategic points around their village and when Drogon and Valtok were seen approaching, they hid their wives and children and set fire to their own dwellings. By the time the brothers came upon the destruction, the area was nothing more than a smoking pile of cinders. Many of the Scaggy lay scattered among the debris pretending to be dead, some had even scorched their clothes and singed their tusks to make sure everything looks convincing.'

'They told how a fearsome warlord had torched their homes and taken their families captive. They knew where the warlord was hiding, that it was not far away. They led Drogon and Valtok to a bank of caves at the edge of the forest, but little did the brothers know they were being led into a trap. A pit had been dug at the mouth of one of the caves, the bottom lined with leaves from the Ethaneum tree. When sprinkled with water, Ethaneum leaves produce a fine, white mist, which, when inhaled, causes immediate loss of consciousness.'

'That's what happened to me,' Tom exclaimed, remembering the white mist that had knocked him out when he tried to reach Badger on the slope. 'Then the Scaggy put me in a cage and hauled me to their camp.'

'The Scaggy are cowards,' Fergil said. 'They only confront those who are rendered helpless. Though they are timid creatures who only attack the weak and vulnerable, their evil nature makes them feed off the misfortunes of others. You are lucky to have escaped them.'

'Once the pit was in place, the Scaggy covered it with branches and twigs then threw a layer of earth over the top to make it look like solid ground. When Drogon and Valtok stepped onto it, they plunged headlong into the trap. When they were both rendered unconscious they were hauled to the top then bound hand and foot and dragged deep into the forest. Drogon was given over to the Scaggy, who took great delight in torturing him. Valtok was forced to watch.'

'When all life appeared to have left him, they tossed what remained of Drogon's body into a stinking quagmire known as the Bogfen, an area inhabited by giant Jebmoks - slimy squidlings that feed off rotting flesh.'

Lowering his eyes, Fergil started to tremble. 'Hidden from view, I witnessed these evil deeds. When Grod and the Scaggy had gone, I gathered my people and together we pulled Drogon from the mire. Remarkably, he was still alive, but how we managed to keep the flicker of life burning, I will never know. We put him in a cart, covered him with straw and brought him back to the castle, where we have cared for him ever since.' A tear suddenly dripped from the end of Fergil's nose. 'He saved us you see. After we were captured and enslaved, Drogon rescued us and set us free. Now he is a broken man, and so ashamed of his horrific appearance that he allows no one to look upon him.'

'When he recovered, desperate to preserve his dignity, he sought a way of preventing anyone from entering the castle grounds. For this purpose, he called upon the ancient men of magic, who use their talents for the good of Keeros. They provided Drogon with two enormous, bronze warriors to guard the castle gates. Messengers were sent far and wide to spread stories of the horrors that lurk within these walls, horrors that do not exist, that were invented purely to keep prying eyes away. Until now, no one has ever tried to enter these lands.

106

'But what of Valtok?' Tom said. 'What happened to him?'

'Valtok was chained to a tree, close to the cave where the warlord had set up camp. He was starved of food and water and regularly beaten. It was Grod's way of destroying his spirit and at the same time, amusing the hateful Scaggy. Then one day a mighty storm erupted. Thunder boomed across the sky and lightening ripped into the forest, igniting the trees into a mass of roaring flame. Grod and the Scaggy retreated deep into the safety of the caves, leaving Valtok to the mercy of the elements. But by some extraordinary miracle, a lightening fork struck the chains binding his wrists, snapping the links apart and setting him free. Weak with hunger, parched with thirst, he stumbled through the forest in a daze. But when he reached the edge of the woodland, he saw his horse tethered to a tree - a tree that had miraculously escaped the flames.'

'He arrived at the castle draped limply over the animal's back. He was rambling incoherently and so fired with fever he didn't know where he was. It took a long time to return him to health, and only when he was well enough, did we tell him of Drogon's survival. We tried to prepare him for what he was about to witness, tried to ease the blow, but all he cared about was that his brother was alive. When we took him to Drogon's quarters and he saw the terrible damage that had been done, Valtok broke down and wept.'

'Consumed with hatred and vowing revenge, he returned to the burnt out embers of the forest. He scoured every inch of it, searched the abandoned caves where Grod had been hiding. He combed rivers, streams, hills and mountains, any place he thought the warlord might have taken refuge. But no trace of him was ever found. Eventually Valtok returned to the castle and from that day to this he has kept the army on alert, praying for the moment he can exert his revenge.'

107

. 'I can see now why he detests the Scaggy!' Tom said. 'But how is it they are living here in the castle grounds after causing so much suffering?'

'When the evil warlord abandoned them, they were left to fend for themselves, and as news of Drogon's torture spread, they became objects of hatred and derision. They were hunted down, flushed from every place they sought refuge, driven from every corner of the land. Finally, when there was nowhere left for them to go, they came here to seek Drogon's forgiveness. When he saw how much they had suffered he offered them sanctuary within the castle grounds. All he asked in return was their pledge to lead peaceful, trouble free lives.'

'When Valtok returned he was furious and certain they would deceive Drogon again, demanded they be turned out. But Drogon refused. There was nowhere left for them to go he reasoned, and as long as they remained within the confines of the castle, they would be unable to harm anyone else. He did however make one concession: If the Scaggy were found in any part of the castle grounds other than their designated area, or anywhere else on Keeros, Valtok was sanctioned to deal with them as he saw fit.'

'Though he honours his brother's wishes, Valtok loathes and despises the Scaggy. If they go beyond their defined boundaries or do anything to threaten Drogon's safety, he executes them without question. Those are his rules , , , the Scaggy are fully aware of the consequences of breaking them.'

'Is that what he will do with me?' Tom said. 'Execute me without question?'

'I do not know!' Fergil sighed. 'Valtok is not a wicked man, but his passion to protect his brother is beyond limit, and right now, he is convinced you are here to kill Drogon.'

'But that's not true! He's wrong! I have not come to kill Drogon . . . all I need is to get away . . . before it's too late.'

'Too late?' Fergil frowned. 'Too late for what?' Rising to his feet and made his way across the dungeon floor. 'If you tell me,' he whispered, his huge hooded eyes peering deep into Tom's, '. . . I may be able to help,'

'They sent you to trick me, didn't they?' Tom shouted, remembering how the blue dwarf had deceived him.

'No' Fergil gasped. 'I'm trying to help you.'

'The only way you can help,' Tom cried, jabbing his finger towards the dungeon door, 'is to get me out of here. I must reach Delnar before . . .' Then he stopped, suddenly realising he had revealed his destination something the wizard had forbidden him to do. 'I didn't mean . . I meant.

But it was too late. Fergil was disappearing through the little arched doorway without even a backward glance.

'No! Wait!'

Tom was overwhelmed by a nauseating sense of failure. Why couldn't he have kept his big mouth shut? He paced backwards and forwards, the heavy chain attached to his ankle clanking against the cold, stone flags. Hating himself for what he had just done he threw back his head and cried out in frustration. Then he suddenly fell silent . . . his eyes glaring at the shafts of light streaming through the gaps at the top of the tower. Could he break out his shackles, climb the wall and squeeze through? But as he stared at the huge slabs of stone, his gaze moving across the damp patches of mildew clinging to the surface like leeches, the shiny blobs of water dripping from the edges, he knew he would never make it to the top. Flopping to the floor he drew his knees up to his chest and gazed around the silent, empty space - the rumpled bales of straw - the flickering candle enhancing his solitude. Then, suddenly swinging around, he stared at the little wooden door Fergil had used to enter the dungeon . . . maybe he could get through there.

He grabbed the chain and lifting it from the floor, slid his hands slowly along every link, his fingers searching for one that might not be fully closed. When he found what he was looking for he tugged with all his might until his knuckles turned white and his hands were trembling. Gasping for breath he paused to wipe the sweat from his forehead. Then he tried again and again and again. But no matter how hard he tugged, the link just would not budge. Finally, hot, sweaty and heaving with exhaustion he slumped to the floor in defeat. 'I've got to get out,' he cried. 'I've got to get out.'

But as he sat there quivering, feeling more alone and dejected than ever, he heard the rhythmic thud of marching footsteps - a precise, repeated tempo - like the soul-less ticking of a clock. They grew louder and louder, closer and closer and when they stopped outside his cell, he tensed.

Suddenly the door burst open and Valtok swept in followed by two armed guards. 'Bring him,' he bellowed, his voice so loud it echoed around the damp, stone walls. Grabbing Tom's arms, the soldiers removed his shackles then frogmarched him out of the door.

Valtok led the way through a labyrinth of passageways, where flickering wall torches reminded Tom of the dismal tunnels beneath the forest. I might as well be back there he thought, for all the good I have done.

After climbing several flights of steps they crossed a covered walkway which took them into the main body of the castle, the musty, lifeless air and bleak, eerie silence crawling across Tom's skin like invisible spiders. When they moved into the great hall, the echo of their footsteps resonated around the startling bare walls, making him wonder how anyone could possibly live in such a place. Finally, they turned into a passageway, pulling to a halt in front of an immense stone wall.

Valtok strode forward and when he pressed his hand against one of the slabs part of the wall slid back, revealing a narrow entrance. Tom was marched into a vast chamber, so far removed in appearance to what he had just seen, he gasped. Three of the walls were covered with shields engraved with ornate coats of arms, beneath each shield hung a lustrous silver sword glimmering under the gentle glow of candlelight. Across from the entrance stood a beautifully decorated door with intricate carvings and shiny brass inlays. The wall surrounding the door was embossed with thousands of names etched in gold, and above them, written in

111

elaborately detailed script were the words, 'Noble Order of Zengal.'

Valtok moved forward and carefully twisting the brass handle, gently eased the door open.

Tom was led into a room of palatial proportions, where richly woven tapestries adorned the walls and crystal chandeliers hung resplendently from the vaulted ceiling. Sculptured effigies of mounted warriors lined the edges of the room, their images mirrored in the gleaming marble floor like trees reflected in a lake. As they made their way past columns of polished granite, rising high above them like great gothic monoliths, Tom noticed that Valtok's demeanour had softened, he was now walking reverently, treading softly on coloured prisms of light reflected from the enormous stained glass windows.

When they reached a small doorway on the other side of the room, the soldiers pulled to a halt. Valtok drew a long, deep breath and when the guards moved into position, one at either side of the entrance, he pushed the door open then yanked Tom inside.

They entered a darkened room heavy with stale air and the odour of candle-wax. There were no windows that Tom could see, no light other than that radiating from a blazing log fire and a candle flickering at the side of an enormous hearth. In front of the hearth, with its back facing Tom stood a large winged armchair.

As he gazed around the room, transfixed by the soothing aura of calm, he noticed something stir at the edge of his vision. Turning his head, he saw a figure silhouetted against the dim light moving softly across the floor. When it entered the glow of the fire, he instantly recognised Fergil.

'My master, Drogon, wishes to speak with you,' the creature said, his voice no louder than a whisper. 'He wishes to know why you are here. Who sent you?' Crooking a long, spindly finger, he beckoned Tom forward. 'Please . . . take a seat by the fire.'

'No!' Tom cried, stiffening his body. 'I will tell him nothing.'

A rush of cold air suddenly whooshed past his head. Then he felt the tip of Valtok's sword press hard into his back. 'He's been sent to kill you!' the warrior bellowed.

From the other side of the armchair came a weary, rasping voice. 'Brother . . . put away your sword.'

'There can be no other reason for his presence. When he talks of Delnar he lies! Why would a mere boy go there?'

'We do not know until we speak with him. What we do know, is that he would not put his life in jeopardy without good reason. Maybe he is afraid to tell us what that reason is.'

'There's nothing to tell! He's here to kill you! He should be executed like the filthy Scaggy.'

Ignoring his brother's bitterness, Drogon leaned forward. Tom could tell by the sudden, sharp intake of breath that he was in pain. 'At least move into the firelight where I can see you,' he breathed.

'No!' Valtok thundered, barring his way. 'He'll kill you!'

'Then to ensure my safety, you will stand by me. Come here young man and sit by the fire. It has been a long time . . . perhaps too long . . . since I enjoyed conversation.

Tom glared starkly into Valtok's angry eyes and determined for once to get the better of the obnoxious beast, he squeezed past his gigantic body and plonked himself down on a stool at the side of the hearth. When he glanced towards the winged armchair he saw a hunched figure covered by a long, dark robe, the face hidden beneath the hood, the hands concealed by copious folds of sleeve and the feet tucked away inside a deep layer of cloth draped neatly against the floor.

'Have you come to kill me as the Scaggy claim?' Drogon whispered.

Surprised by the gentle warmth of the voice, Tom answered with a nervous stutter. 'N . . . No,' he said.

'Then why are you here?'

'The Scaggy took me prisoner, they were going to roast me alive. But I escaped and made them take me back to where they found me. When we were captured by the soldiers, the Scaggy said I was forcing them to lead me to the castle - that I wanted to kill you. But that wasn't true. They were lying.'

'How did you get into the castle grounds? Drogon asked. 'Where were you going?' If you were trying to reach Delnar as you say, I would like to know why. Only those seeking Zafror, the element of fire, would go there.'

Tom felt a shudder of uncertainty. Though the wizard had instructed him to tell no one of his mission, he knew Valtok was ready to annihilate him if he didn't answer. Should he risk disclosing the reason for being sent there? But if he did . . . what would happen then? Bracing himself, he took a deep breath and staring at the shrouded figure said, 'I cannot reveal my mission to anyone.'

'Mission? Then someone must have sent you. Are you in some kind of trouble? If so I may be able to help.'

'I wish you could,' Tom sighed, 'But I doubt it.'

'If you don't tell me, then how will I know?'

'I can't tell anyone. I promised.'

'But you can trust me. You need not fear me.'

'What I fear,' Tom said, his mind racked with indecision, 'is that my mission will fail. I must get to Delnar . . . before it's too late.'

'Then tell me about it,' Drogon sighed. 'How can I help you if I don't know?'

Tom lowered his head and covering his face with his hands, he shuddered. He didn't know what to do. He didn't know what they were going to do with him. Without any hope of escape his mission to recover the Charquery Key was bound to fail and if that was the case, what difference would it make if he told Drogon where he was going and why. Raising his head, he stared at the silent figure hunched in the armchair. Then he whispered, 'I don't suppose it matters anymore who I tell. By now it's probably too late.'

'Then let us hear it.' Drogon said. 'Let it out.'

Tom could see nothing beyond the many folds of the dark robe, but as he gazed at the silent figure he felt something stir inside - something he could not explain - something that was telling him Drogon could indeed be trusted.

'I am not from your world,' he said at last. 'I was summoned here by Altair Devole, to help save Keeros from destruction.'

Little by little his story unfolded. He told of his life on earth and how Norva had transported him to Keeros. He explained his mission to retrieve the Charquery key, how vital it was that he reached Delnar to seek Zafror's help, and the consequences should he fail to return the key to the Everlasting Tree in time. He told of the Pit of Pendurak and its power over Arcos, his terrifying encounters with Scavrad, the Grybb and the Skrorth. Finally, as his voice began to tremble and his eyes filled with tears, he spoke of Badger. 'I don't know where he is,' he cried. 'The last time I saw him was in the forest. I don't know if he's been captured, killed, or eaten by the Scaggy.' Filled with despair, he lowered his head and wept.

A strange stillness had descended on the small, stuffy room. No sound could be heard except for the crackle and hiss of the fire. Then a mocking laugh suddenly penetrated the silence. 'How can anyone believe this nonsense?' Valtok roared, the words spitting angrily from his mouth. 'He lies!'

'I'm not lying,' Tom yelled. 'It's true.'

'If it's true, then you need to prove it. But you can't. Can you? Because you were not heading for Delnar at all, you came here for one reason and one reason only. To kill my brother!'

'Stop!' Drogon shouted, his faltering breath gushing out in one long gasp. 'There is a way Tom can prove what he says is true.' Leaning towards him, still hidden by the many folds of his robe, he whispered, 'You say Altair Devole sent you?'

'Yes,' Tom nodded.

'And he wants you to enter Delnar?'

'Yes.'

116

'No one can enter Delnar unless they carry the seal of the eastern wizard. And even then, it would have to be for a matter of life or death. If Altair Devole did indeed send you, he would have given you a bronze medallion - the only means by which you could enter Delnar safely.'

The seal . . . Tom had forgotten.

'Yes!' he shouted, jumping to his feet. 'I can prove I'm telling the truth. It's here!' Tearing his shirt open he grinned at the simplicity of the solution. But Valtok was not smiling, neither was Fergil, and Drogon remained passively unmoved. Tom glanced quickly from one to the other - he couldn't understand what was wrong - then he looked down at his chest. The seal was gone.

'That's it!' Valtok growled, shaking his fist. 'I knew he was lying.'

'No wait! It was here! Believe me it was!'

Striding forward, the huge warrior swept Tom from the floor and threw him over his shoulder. 'You've had your chance,' he roared, marching towards the door. 'Now you will die.'

'Wait!' Fergil cried, leaping across the room so fast he almost fell into the fire. 'What's that?' Running to the doorway he blocked Valtok's path, then pointed to a piece of broken chain hanging from the neck of Tom's shirt. 'Please,' he begged as the warrior shuddered to a halt. 'Just take a look.'

Turning his head, Valtok saw the thread of broken chain and wrapping his fingers around it, jerked his wrist and gave it a mighty tug. When it flew from the top of Tom's shirt, the warrior held it up for all to see. It was empty. Valtok's eyes glowed with anger. Growling like an angry bear he glared at

117

Fergil. But as he started to march away, something clattered to the floor.

'It's here,' Fergil cried, snatching the bronze medallion up. 'Look!'

Frowning suspiciously, Valtok grabbed the seal from Fergil's outstretched hand. Turning it over and over in his fingers he carefully examined the symbols etched into the surface, then read the strange archaic words inscribed along the edge. Drawing a deep, shuddering breath he raised his head slowly and lifting Tom from his shoulders placed him gently on the floor. Staring the boy straight in the eye, he said, 'Long ago the eastern wizard saved my life. He sent great lightening forks from the sky, releasing me from the brutality of an evil warlord. He would entrust this seal to no one without good reason. This medallion suggests grave danger. It also proves my suspicions of you are unfounded. I have wronged you boy. If my brother agrees, I will right this wrong.'

Tom felt a huge wave of relief sweep through him as he watched Valtok stride towards his brother. Turning his head, he looked around the darkened room for Fergil, who was standing quietly beside the door. 'Thanks.' He whispered.

The creature came a few paces forward and squeezing Tom's shoulder said. 'I'm really glad you're okay. Let's hope they can figure out what to do.' Then, with a slight wave of his spindly hand, he moved back to the door and slipped quietly from the room.

'I will escort Tom to Delnar,' Valtok said, pacing backwards and forwards in front of Drogon. 'The special guard will remain behind for your protection. Once the boy's task on the mountain is complete, I will take the main body of the army and ride to Bragenon Forest. We will defeat Arcos together.'

Scarcely believing his ears, Tom stared open mouthed at the gigantic warrior who, only moments ago wanted nothing less than to lop off his head. Moving closer he said, 'With you on my side, I'm certain of success. I only hope we can get the key back in time.'

'We have strong, fast horses,' Valtok grinned, slapping Tom on the back with such enthusiasm he sent him skidding across the floor. 'We'll soon make up for the time that's been lost.'

No one noticed Fergil slip back into the room. Moving to the rear of the winged armchair he stood quietly behind it waiting for the conversation to end. He didn't have long to wait, for several moments later, when plans had been agreed, Valtok strode towards the door. 'Come on lad,' he called. 'Let's get going!'

As they made their way out of the room, Fergil crept up behind Tom and tapped him on the shoulder. When the boy swung around, his eyes burst wide and he let out a startled gasp. Badger was sitting in Fergil's arms.

'Wow!' Tom exclaimed. 'Where did you find him?'

'I found him wandering in the woods. I brought him here to save him from the Scaggy.'

After ordering his army to prepare for battle, Valtok escorted Tom and a very excited Badger into the courtyard, where a gleaming chestnut horse was stamping its hooves impatiently on the cobbled floor. The animal looked magnificent, its sleek copper coat smooth and shiny, its eyes beaming like jewels.

'He's fast and sure.' Valtok said, sliding his hand across the horse's muscular flank. 'That's why we named him Swift. He's one of our finest. And he's all yours.'

'Mine!' Tom exclaimed, patting the horse's neck. 'Wow! . . . Now I know I can make it.'

'Not without this!' Valtok grinned, casting a covetous eye over Tom's sword. 'It would have been mine should you have perished.' Sliding the weapon into its scabbard, he handed it to Tom, smiling as he watched him fasten it around his waist. Then he slapped him on the back and hoisted him into the saddle. 'And you'll need this to tame the Spineclaw,' he said, sliding the wizard's medallion over the boy's head. 'I've fixed the broken link.'

As they were about to leave, Tom heard a clatter of hooves coming from the other end of the courtyard. Shading his eyes from the sun, he saw Fergil, accompanied by six mounted soldiers, trotting towards him on a sleek black horse.

'He insisted on coming.' Valtok chuckled. 'There's no way he would let us leave without him.'

Tom smiled as the scrawny creature pulled up beside him. 'Thanks Fergil,' he said. 'If it wasn't for you, I don't know what would have happened.'

When Valtok mounted his horse, his scarlet cloak falling loosely over the animal's gleaming flanks, he swung towards the gateway and thrust his arm into the air. At that moment the enormous portcullis started rumbling open, and when the gap was large enough to pass through, they all moved out of the courtyard and headed down the slope towards the woodland.

'The main body of the army is waiting for us at the castle gates,' Valtok said as they trotted along a narrow, dusty path. 'When you have done what you need to do on the mountain, we ride to Bragenon forest.'

They rode through the woods until they arrived at the place where Tom had been captured by the Scaggy. Valtok led the way up the slope and after pushing through the trees at the top, they came to the castle wall. Ordering the others to remain behind, he jumped from his horse, opened the concealed entrance then escorted Tom through.

'Swift will carry you as far as he can,' he said, remounting his horse, 'but as the medallion's power extends only to you and Badger, I will soon have to bring him back. When that time comes, I will wait for you below.'

Because he was the one in possession of the medallion, Tom had to take the lead as they moved up the narrow shingle track - if they encountered the Spineclaw, he would have to show the seal pretty quickly. They progressed at a steady pace, but when they were half way up the mountain, Tom felt the muscles in Swift's flanks tighten and a jerky stiffness enter his step. The horse seemed tense and wary, his teeth clenched tight against the pull of the bit, his eyes wide and staring. Suddenly, without warning, he threw his head and reared.

'What's wrong boy?' Valtok called, watching the jittery animal prancing up and down.

'Something must have spooked him.' Tom cried.

 Moving closer, Valtok grabbed hold of Swift's reins. 'Steady boy. Steady.' As the petrified horse pounded its hooves, sending an avalanche of pebbles cascading down the narrow track, he gazed cautiously round. 'He senses the Spineclaw. From here you must go on foot. I'll take Swift and wait for you below.' Struggling to keep the panicked animal from bolting, he waited for Tom to dismount then hurried away. 'Be sure to keep the seal in full view,' he shouted, slithering quickly down the slope.

Tom made sure the medallion was on the outside of his jacket, but as he watched the warrior descend, disappearing every now and then behind clusters of jagged rock, he suddenly felt an overwhelming sense of isolation. Apart from Badger, who was pressing his shivering body against his leg, he was now completely alone, and he felt further away from anyone than he had ever felt in his life. 'Come on Badger,' he whispered, his stomach churning like a mill wheel. 'Let's go.'

Holding the medallion in one hand and grasping the hilt of his sword with the other, he started up the steep, shingle path, moving as fast as the rugged ground would allow. They hadn't gone far when they came to a ledge jutting beyond the natural slope of the mountain. Above it, a crystal clear waterfall tumbled into an enormous rocky basin. Tom quickly scanned the area then lifting Badger onto the ledge,

122

scrambled up behind. He glanced around again to make sure all was well, then kneeling down, pulled the map from his sock. After spreading it carefully on the ground he ran his finger along the red line leading from the bottom of the mountain to the waterfall. There he saw a note written in bright, blue ink, confirming what Goodstad had told him to do:

'At the tumbling fall look for the Stellusaris plant, it has white flowers with petals shaped like birds. Before you go any further, you must inhale its heady scent to protect you from the heat of the mountain. Once this is done move quickly into the tunnel behind the flow, which leads into a vast crater. At the centre of the crater stands the firerock. Place the seal upon it to alert Zafror of your presence, but you must do it quickly, before Traak, the Keeper of Delnar awakes.'

Folding the map, he pushed it quickly down his sock then looked around for the plant he was supposed to sniff. He saw a cluster of pearly white flowers with tiny petals shaped like birds peeping from the side of the ledge. Scrambling over the rock he snapped off two stems then hurrying back to Badger, shoved one under his nose and one under his own. As the little dog sniffed, Tom inhaled the most beautiful aroma he had ever encountered, but as it wafted through his senses, he suddenly turned icy cold and started to shiver. 'Come on,' he said, staring at the remains of Badger's mangled flower. 'This stuff's working pretty fast. Let's go.'

Pushing his own flower into his pocket, he slithered behind the waterfall into a long, dark, passageway, where the sound of water gushing over rock echoed through the silence. Seeing daylight glowing at the other end of the tunnel he hurried towards it as fast as he could, occasionally bumping into Badger as his feet skidded on the damp, uneven ground.

When he eventually burst into the open, he found himself standing in an enormous, rocky crater, its huge jagged walls resembling the top of an extinct volcano. A blazing rock was standing at the centre.

A shiver suddenly streaked down his spine. Something was watching him. He could feel it. Gazing around the vast crater walls he searched for gaps large enough to hide a dragon, but all he could see were narrow cracks and crevices, openings that looked like small caves - nothing big enough to conceal a gigantic beast. Yet the hair on the back of his neck was standing on end, his heart beating so fast it felt like a time bomb. 'Don't be stupid,' he whispered to himself. 'There's nothing here.' Lifting Badger into his arms he grasped the medallion tight between his fingers and raced for the firerock.

When he reached the blazing stone, he saw that to place the seal into the hollow at the top, he needed to push his hand through the raging wall of fire dancing across its surface. As his heart began to thud he yanked the Stellusaris flower from his pocket and took another hefty sniff. Placing Badger on the ground he pulled the medallion carefully over his head. Then holding his breath, he thrust his arm directly into the flame. He gasped when he saw his skin turn bright red and trembled when he felt his wrist being squeezed as if held in a vice. But he couldn't feel any heat.

The instant the seal dropped into the hollow an earth-shattering rumble came from deep within the mountain. Suddenly the crater walls started glowing, shaking and trembling as an avalanche of fragmented stone crashed to the ground. Then, as the rock face expanded, heaving slowly in and out as though it were breathing, Tom watched in horror as a massive, two-headed beast tore itself from the stone. Lashing its tail from side to side, its razor sharp talons splayed like knives, the massive Gavad Spineclaw let out a spine chilling roar, sending jets of searing flame shooting across the sky.

With every nerve and sinew in his body quaking Tom grabbed the seal from the rock and thrust it out. Suddenly the monstrous beast lunged forward, its two snarling heads stopping inches from his face, its fiery red eyes glaring at the medallion dangling in his trembling fingers. He stood there motionless, his breath held fast, his heart thudding with fear.

At that moment a girl emerged from a crevice in the crater wall. She moved hurriedly through the haze, her auburn hair falling loose against the folds of her vivid, orange cloak, her delicate white skin glowing with incandescence. She looked miniscule against the hugeness of the great, hulking beast but as she drew near, gesturing the angry creature to draw back, it suddenly thudded its huge, scaly body to the ground, its two enormous heads grumbling and complaining.

'You come from the eastern wizard?' she gasped, her gaze moving to the gleaming medallion swinging in Tom's hand. 'Then Keeros must be in danger.'

'It is!' Tom exclaimed. 'We need Zafror's help!'

'Then I will take you to him,' she said. 'Quick, follow me.'

Tom hesitated at the thought of moving past the enormous, brooding beast. It could shred him to pieces with just one swipe of its razor sharp claws and the threatening glare of its fiery red eyes had never left his face. 'Will it let me pass?' he grimaced.

'Traak will not harm you,' the girl smiled. 'Come, we must hurry.'

125

Hoisting Badger over his shoulder Tom raced past the Spineclaw as though escaping a swarm of angry bees. When he was half way across the crater a deafening roar thundered through the air. Without stopping to look back he ran even faster, his breath puffing out in short, sharp gasps. As soon as he reached the rock face he swung around. The girl had pulled to a halt and was glaring into the monstrous creature's eyes. She looked like a tiny speck against its hulking, great body, but her finger was wagging and her head moving sharply from side to side. As she turned to walk away the creature slumped down and snorted miserably.

'He's just showing off,' she said when she caught up with Tom, 'trying to impress you with his power. He doesn't seem to realise just how alarming he can be.'

The creature's dragon-like heads were now flattened to the ground, grumbling and growling as though in disgrace, but its fiery red eyes were still fixed hard on Tom. A shudder ran down his spine as he placed Badger on the ground, then, taking one, final look at the enormous Gavad Spineclaw, he followed the girl through a narrow fissure in the crater wall.

They entered a large, rocky cave where the tinny smell of molten metal filled the air and a thumping, droning noise came from somewhere deep within the mountain. It must have been very hot, because Tom's skin instantly turned red and his nose and eyes felt dry.

As they moved down a sloping tunnel where tongs of searing flame flared from the top of the walls, he told her who he was, where he had come from and who had sent him. He explained his mission to retrieve the Charquery key and the consequences should he fail to return it to the Everlasting tree in time.

126

'My father Zafror has great power,' she smiled. 'He will help you.'

***When they reached the core of the mountain they came to a circular metal door set into an enormous wall of rock. As the girl moved towards it, the door swung slowly open. Gesturing Tom to follow, she led him into a vast underground cavern. A dry tinge of heat stung his eyes as he watched blasts of searing flame leap up from the white stone walls. When the flames reached the roof space, they danced across a canopy of glistening rock studded with thousands of dazzling red crystals.

'This is firestone,' the girl said. 'It exists only in Delnar and has many special powers.'

'Wow,' Tom gasped, his eyes wide with amazement 'Do you live here?'

'Yes,' she smiled. 'But as I am born of the element of fire, from a time before creation, my natural state of being is very different from what you see. To you I appear in a form you can easily recognise.'

'Oh!' Tom muttered, wondering what she really looked like.

He followed her across the cavern until they reached a pyramid shaped structure constructed of thick granite. Leading him through the heavy door she said, 'You must stay in here until I return. Do not leave the safety of this shelter. It will give you protection.' With that she hurried away and when she closed the door behind her, Tom found himself engulfed in a dark, noiseless void, the only light coming from a narrow slit set half way up the wall.

Wondering what he needed to be protected from, he lifted Badger into his arms and peered through the narrow opening.

He saw the girl running across the cavern floor pulling the hood of her cloak over her head. As she approached the centre, a crimson flame shot into the air, mushrooming across the roof and walls like an enormous fiery umbrella. His eyes grew wide as he watched the flame engulf her, changing from red to yellow then yellow to orange until it blended exactly with the colour of her cloak. At that moment, she vanished.

***Suddenly a whirl of silver mist flooded the cavern, growing thicker and thicker until the orange flame could no longer been seen. Then, as a fountain of dazzling sparks exploded into the air, a radiant figure rose from the ground, its light was so bright, so glaringly white, Tom had to jerk his head away to the safety of the shelter. As he slid to the floor, blinking to clear the glare from his vision, a shaft of light shot through the narrow gap, making him jump so hard he almost toppled over. Pushing Badger under his jacket he stayed absolutely still, his mouth gaping wide as he watched the dazzling beam move up the wall. When it reached the pyramid's apex it grew dimmer, gradually expanding into a soft arc of light, then, moving slowly down again, it stopped at the place where Tom was crouching. Resting on his face, it magnified the fear in his wide, startled eyes.

It was then he heard a noise. Puffing the air from his lungs in one long gasp, he swung his head to the right. The girl was standing in the doorway, her body silhouetted against the light, her eyes shimmering like stars. 'Don't be alarmed,' she said. 'Zafror will not harm you.' Lifting Badger from Tom's arms she placed him on the ground then reaching down, gently stroked the little dog's head. 'Stay here, where you will be safe,' she smiled. 'Tom, you must come with me.'

When he left the safety of the shelter, he saw the glowing, luminous figure, which had risen so startlingly from the ground, cloaked by the swirling silver mist, its light subdued enough for him to be able to see without being dazzled. When they reached the edge of the silver mist, Tom felt a powerful force of emerging pulsating all around. Shuddering, he pulled to a stop behind the girl.

'We can go no further,' she said, turning towards him. 'Zafror wishes to communicate. But to do so, he must enter your mind. Do not be afraid.' Placing her hand on his shoulder, she gazed directly into his deep brown eyes. Unable to look away, he felt a strange dizziness whirl around his head, then, still feeling the throb of energy pulsing all around, he drifted into a deep, hypnotic trance.

As the sounds of the cavern receded, a rush of icy wind brushed his skin and as darkness descended all around, he saw a circle of red light hurtling towards him. Within seconds he was surrounded by a mass of screeching demons, their writhing forms and hideous snarls making him cry out with fear. To his right a band of Skrorth were hissing and spitting, in their midst the blue dwarf brandished a bloodstained silver arrow. Suddenly a terrifying howl rang through the darkness. Looking down Tom saw a pack of snarling Grybb circling his feet. From the head of one of the beasts rose a sinister, black snake, its forked tongue lashing in and out, its evil, orange eyes glaring directly into his. When it drew level with his shoulders it slithered around his body, coiling so tight he felt the air being squeezed from his lungs. Then he saw Arcos moving towards him, his ghastly eyes radiating a wild, demonic glare. At that moment a piercing screech sounded from above and as the gigantic Skrell swooped down, sweeping low over the band of shrieking demons, they suddenly disintegrated to nothing.

When the bird thudded to the ground, its gigantic form towering high over Tom's head, a ring of coloured light began swirling around its body, whirling so fast it became a thick, hazy blur. Then the Skrell too was gone, in its place stood Lyal, a silver bow slung over his shoulder. Behind him, Tom could see Altair Devole and Norva. He tried to call out, tried to tell them what was happening, but no sound would come from his lips. As they drifted away he was confronted with a memory from the deepest recesses of his mind - an old man sitting alone on a hillside gazing across a snow covered winter valley.

Suddenly Tom was back in the cavern and as if waking from a terrifying dream, let out a long, shuddering cry.

'Zafror has been one with your mind,' the girl whispered. 'He has seen the horrors you have seen, the terrors you have faced and witnessed the pain you have endured. Now he will give you the power you seek - the power to defeat Arcos.' Suddenly a jet of flame shot through the silver mist. 'Do not be afraid,' the girl said, catching Tom's arm as he leapt out of the way. 'You are safe.' Like a whirl of burning wind the flame engulfed him, spiralling up until it covered the top of his head. There was no heat - no pain - all he could feel was a warm breeze brushing his face and limbs. Then, as quickly as it had appeared the fire receded, leaving a piece of dazzling red crystal spinning at his feet.

'As long as this firestone is in your possession,' the girl said, 'the power of Zafror is at your fingertips.'

'What will it do?' Tom gasped, his fingers trembling as he lifted the crystal from the ground.

'It will protect you from the evil of Pendurak and give you the means of retrieving the Charquery Key. Come, we must hurry. Time is running out.'

***After collecting Badger from the shelter, Tom followed the girl across the cavern. The radiant figure surrounded by silver mist had vanished, the vibrating pulse of energy had gone and the centre of the floor had returned to solid stone.

'When you reach Arcos's fortress,' she said, as they made their way out of the mountain,' point the firestone directly at the Grybb guarding the entrance. It will render them helpless and allow you to pass in safety. No one will be able to harm you as long as you are holding the crystal. Once you have passed through the tunnel, make your way to the ice block, touch it with the firestone and the Charquery Key will be released. You must then move quickly to the pit and throw the firestone directly into its depths. Once this is done, ride as fast as you can to the Everlasting tree, where the Eastern wizard will be waiting. Only when the portal is unlocked, will our worlds be safe.'

They emerged from the mountain through a heavy stone door situated close to the castle wall. 'Thanks for this,' Tom said, pushing the crystal into his pocket. 'With the firestone and the help of Valtok's army, I know I can succeed.'

'Take care,' the girl said, 'and be sure to keep the firestone with you at all times, do not let it out of your sight.' She pointed down a narrow lane. 'The gateway is just over there.'

When Tom reached the bottom of the path, he saw Fergil standing by the gate holding the horses. 'Where's Valtok?' he shouted 'Wait 'til he sees what I've got!'

Fergil's expression was grave. 'We've been invaded. It's the warlord, Grod. He's been sighted in the north leading a massive army. Valtok suspects he's behind the plot to destroy Keeros, and has taken the Zengal army to stop him.

He asked me to ride with you, to help you with your task. If all goes well, he will meet us in Bragenon forest.'

'Let's hope he makes it back in time,' Tom said, feeling his heart sink as he climbed into the saddle. 'Come on Fergil. Let's go.'

When they reached the castle gates, Tom was relieved to find that two of Valtok's soldiers had been sent to ensure their safe passage between the sentinels. 'Any news of Valtok?' he asked, pulling Swift to a halt.

'We've heard nothing since he left. Reports say Grod's army is immense.'

'Then we must hurry.' Bending down, Tom scooped Badger from the ground and draped him across the withers of his horse. 'Come on Fergil. We must ride like the wind!'

With the frantic rumble of hooves pounding the dusty earth, they galloped through the woodland then out into the blistering heat of the open plain, their eyes stinging with the force of air pushing against their faces. But not until they had reached the slope leading to Bragenon Forest, did they slow their horses to give them chance to catch their breath.

'What happened on the mountain?' Fergil panted, trying to fill his lungs with huge gulps of air. 'Did you see the Spineclaw?'

'Oh yes!' Tom gasped, his eyes growing wide. 'He's part of the mountain, part of the Skrellk. He's got two heads and a body bigger than anything you've ever seen. And he breathes fire - masses and masses of it. If it hadn't been for the medallion he would have killed me for sure.'

'Wow,' Fergil said. 'And Zafror . . . what was he like?'

132

'I didn't see him properly, he was surrounded by silver mist. But I felt his power . . . and believe me, it was staggering. Look!' Tom pulled the glowing red crystal from his pocket.'

'What is it?'

'It's firestone. It holds Zafror's power.'

Badger, who was still draped across Swift's withers like a lumpy sack of potatoes, pricked his ears and turned his head. Thinking the firestone was something tasty, he gave it a few licks, then, maybe because he had ingested some of Zafror's power, his eyes grew large and his tail began to wag. 'Hey!' Tom gasped, yanking the crystal away.

'When I've got the key,' he said, turning back to Fergil. 'I have to throw the firestone right into the heart of Pendurak.'

'Oh,' Fergil said, a worried expression flickering across his face.

Tom knew he was afraid. Who wouldn't be? Gazing into the creature's anxious eyes, he slid the crystal back into his pocket. Then he suddenly gathered his reins and set off up the slope at full gallop. At the top of the rise, where a wide sweep of blackened trees blocked his view, he caught the first odorous waft of Pendurak.

'What happened?' Fergil shouted, struggling to catch up. 'You went like the wind - whoosh, you were gone!'

'I'm going alone,' Tom said, inhaling the putrid stench. 'It's too dangerous. You stay here with Badger.'

'No!' Fergil shouted angrily, 'I'm going with you.'

'You've no idea what's in there. Stay here with Badger.'

133

Moving his horse in front of Toms, Fergil grabbed hold of Swift's reins. 'As you have probably noticed I'm not a brave creature. I would rather be anywhere than here right now. But I am here. And I am here for a purpose. To help you.' He glared defiantly into Tom's startled eyes. 'We go together!'

'But, Badger!' Tom said. 'I can't take him! It's not safe!' He placed the little dog gently on the ground. 'Stay here boy. Don't move until we get back.'

Badger glared up at him, and if Tom hadn't known better, he would have thought the little dog was shaking his head in defiance. Suddenly a deep growl rumbled in the back of Badger's throat and with an angry yap he raced away into the forest.

'It's licking the firestone that's done it,' Tom muttered. 'Come on Fergil, let's go.'

The forest was as silent as a graveyard at the dead of night, its eerie emptiness making the hair on the back of Tom's neck stand on end and goose bumps rise like bubbles on his skin. Though he knew the Skrorth were no longer a threat, he had no idea what other ghastly creatures might be lurking, and kept his eyes constantly trained on the dark, empty spaces between the trees.

Except for the muffled thud of hooves and the intermittent chatter of Fergil's teeth they rode along making hardly a sound, and before long, as a sharp sting of cold gripped their faces, they saw thin patches of ice forming on the ground.

'We're close,' Tom whispered. 'We'll ride in single file. I'll go first, Badger in the middle. When we reach the wall we'll dismount'

134

They rode cautiously through the dark, withering trees and to be sure their progress remained as quiet as it could be, were careful to tread only where the ground was free from ice. As they drew closer to the encampment and the sickening stench of Pendurak poured into their noses, Fergil clamped his hand tight around his mouth to stop himself from retching.

When Tom eventually caught sight of the towering wall of ice surrounding Arcos's fortress he pulled to a halt. Sliding from his horse, he was about to make his way to the edge of the trees, to check how far they were from the entrance, when he heard a groan. It was coming from somewhere behind. Curling his fingers around the hilt of his sword, he swung around.

Fergil's horse was standing by a tree, its head bent to the ground rummaging for food, but Fergil and Badger were nowhere in sight. Leading Swift forward, Tom tethered both horses to a tree branch then sliding his sword from its scabbard, started back through the eerie silence. He hadn't gone far when he heard another groan. It was coming from the other side of a boulder jutting from the edge of the path. He darted around, his eyes swept the forest, then holding his sword ready he crept cautiously around the stone. Fergil was slumped in a heap, his hands clutching the sides of his head, a thin line of blood trickling down his face.

'What happened?' Tom whispered, 'Are you all right?'

'Something hit me from behind. As I fell I saw it push Badger into a sack. Then it hurried away and everything went black. I'm sorry Tom.'

'Which way did it go?'

'It went along there.' Fergil pointed to a frozen pathway bending away to the right.

'Stay here,' Tom said. 'I'm going for Badger.'

Careful not to make a sound, he crept along the edge of the narrow path. When he reached the bend he saw a huge, shaggy coated creature trundling along with a wriggling sack slung over its shoulder. Ducking into the trees he moved steadily forward, but as he drew level with the creature, it suddenly jerked to a stop. Its scabby ears pricked up, its enormous mouth fell open and its shiny black eyes, perched on the ends of two stumpy stalks, fixed directly on the ground. A fat, green toad had landed with a soggy thud close to its feet.

It glared at the croaking animal for several seconds, its gaze held steady. Then a long, black tongue shot from its mouth and with the speed of a bull whip scooped the toad into its huge, crushing jaws. It crunched and chewed and chewed and crunched, then swallowing hard, squeezed its stumpy eyes together and let out a loud, satisfied burp. Turning slowly in a circle it scanned the forest, thick saliva drooling from the corners of its hideous mouth. Then it swung the wriggling sack from its shoulder, flung it to the ground and untying the oily string, plunged its hand inside.

'Arghh!'

The shrillness of its scream almost made the treetops shudder. Roaring with pain it wrenched its hand away and swinging its leg back, gave the sack a hefty kick. Again it thrust its hand inside, this time pulling Badger out by the scruff of his neck. Holding the little dog at arms length it threw back its head then lowered him slowly towards its huge, crushing jaws.

'No!' Tom bellowed, sweeping up his sword as he charged from the trees like a red eyed angry bull.

The startled creature swung around, straight into the path of the gleaming blade and with a sickening thud the arm holding Badger was sliced from its body. There was a moment of stunned shock, its stumpy eyes beat back and forth, its massive feet thudded the earth. Then, snarling with fury it lunged forward. Darting out of its way, Tom ran to grab Badger when suddenly three razor sharp talons sprang from the monster's remaining hand. Bellowing a thunderous roar, it flew at Tom's throat. As he dodged to one side, Badger leapt into its path and toppling it to the ground sent it scudding across the ice like an oversized gorilla. Bouncing along, it suddenly hit a Skrellk and flipping over, landed with a forceful thud, its razor sharp talons knifing its neck. It let out a long, gurgling groan then fell silent.

Tom stared at the lifeless body for several moments, his breath puffing out in short, sharp gasps, his eyes bulging wide. With his sword held ready he crept slowly forward, one faltering step after another, until he was level with the creature's head. 'Ugh,' he gasped, when he saw blood oozing from a gaping wound in its throat.

Sweeping Badger into his arms he raced back through the forest as fast as his legs would carry him.

'What happened?' Fergil yelled, glaring in horror at the glistening blood streaking Tom's clothes. 'What was it?'

'I don't know.' Tom gasped, his voice trembling. 'But it's dead.' Placing Badger on the ground, he helped Fergil to his feet. 'Come on. Let's get out of here.'

The horses were huddled by the tree, the fur on their coats standing on end as great clouds of white steam puffed from their nostrils.

'Are you sure you're all right?' Tom said, seeing the pain on Fergil's face as he hitched him into the saddle. 'I mean . . . you don't have to come . . . you can go back if you like.'

'Thanks,' Fergil smiled weakly. 'I'll be okay.'

Tom crept to the edge of the trees then peered along the curve of the ice wall. There was no sign of the tunnel leading into the encampment.

'Come on,' he whispered, climbing onto his horse. 'We need to go further round.'

They moved through the forest together, Fergil's huge, hooded eyes on the lookout for anything that might want to whack him on the head again, while Badger, badly shaken by being almost eaten alive, trotted so close to Swift's hooves, he was in danger of being kicked in the head. Soon they came into a thick cloud of ground mist that swirled and swayed around the horses' legs, and hearing a succession of vicious snarls coming from somewhere nearby, Fergil started to shiver.

'Stay here,' Tom whispered, pulling Swift to a halt.

He slid lightly from the saddle, careful not to make a sound as he eased himself onto the frozen earth, then crept through the trees. When he was as close to the ice wall as he could get without being seen, he peered out. The tunnel leading into the enclosure stood a little way to the right. In front of it, two ferocious Skrellious Grybb were locked in combat, their huge lumbering bodies heaving to and fro, their heavy neck chains - fastened to huge metal hooks in the wall - clanged and clattered on the ice.

Creeping back to Fergil, Tom remounted his horse. 'Wait here with Badger,' he whispered, mouthing the words almost without sound. 'When it's safe I will signal. If anything goes wrong, ride as fast as you can to the Eastern wizard. Badger knows the way.'

'Good luck,' Fergil mouthed back, trying to keep his hands from trembling and his teeth from chattering.

Drawing a deep breath, Tom slid the firestone from his pocket. It felt warm in his fingers, as though preparing itself for the task in hand. 'Steady,' he whispered, when Swift threw his head and started champing nervously at the bit.

Gripped by the frenzy of battle, the Grybb failed to notice him moving silently through the withered trees towards them, and when he burst into the open, pointing the firestone directly at their snarling faces, it was too late. A dazzling beam of light shot from the firestone, covering the creatures' heads with a blinding arc of light, freezing their snarling faces, immobilising their pounding feet. When the beam split into two, twining and curling around each of their muscular bodies, they started glowing like beacons in a desert. Then, as a high pitched hum filled the silence, they suddenly turned to stone.

'Wow,' Tom whispered.

'Are you all right?' Fergil's eyes were fixed rigidly on the Grybb as he approached.

139

'You should have felt the power,' Tom gasped. 'It was frightening.'

Urging Swift forward, he moved slowly towards the petrified hounds and holding his breath - afraid they might suddenly spring back to life - eased carefully between them. Then he beckoned to the others to follow.

Fergil rode through first, a shudder coursing his spine as he slid quickly between the stone beasts, but Badger, not wanting to appear the slightest bit intimidated, stopped by the head of one of the Grybb and looking up, staring directly into its face, curled back his lips and snarled.

'Come on,' Fergil urged, a nervous quiver vibrating his voice. 'Don't push your luck!'

Soon they were peering from the confines of the ice tunnel, scanning the encampment as far as their restricted view would allow. The pit was still spewing stinking green smoke but the black cloud Tom had seen hovering above it, had vanished. And there was no sign of Arcos or his screeching band of demons. The shelters fringing the enclosure were barred and shuttered, even the watchtowers at the corners of the ice palace stood empty - no shadowy figures lurking.

'This is odd,' Tom whispered, his teeth chattering nervously as he left the safety of the tunnel.

Moving into the open he held the firestone at arms length, his eyes darting from left to right. When satisfied it was safe he signalled the others.

They moved cautiously through the thickening ground mist, the muffled thud of hooves echoing in the eerie silence. When they drew level with the pit they peered through the billowing green smoke towards the ice palace. It looked silent and empty, its crisp, sculptured elegance contrasting starkly with the bleakness of the camp.

'This is strange.' Tom whispered. 'Where is everyone?'

'I don't know.' Fergil said, his lips quivering nervously. 'But I wish we were out of here.'

With a growing sense of unease, they continued on until they reached the block of ice, towering from the mist.

'Something is wrong,' Tom said, staring at the gleaming object lodged deep at its centre. 'Arcos would never leave the key unprotected.'

'Maybe Valtok got here before us. He's taken them all captive. It's the only explanation!'

'Let's hope so,' Tom sighed, gazing around the encampment. 'I'm going for the key. You stay here with Badger. The sooner we get out of here the better.'

He hadn't realised how high the mist had risen until it curled around his head when he slid from his horse. Unable to see further than a few inches, he mentally pictured where he was in relation to the ice block. He set off towards it, the crystal clasped tight between his fingers. Then he suddenly stopped dead. Something was heaving warm, fetid breath against the back of his neck. As he spun around a beam of dazzling light shot from the firestone. But before he could see what was there a heavy blow knocked it from his grasp. Dropping to his knees he followed the glowing light as it slithered across the ice, then another heavy blow sent him crashing to the ground.

Through the galaxy of stars swirling around his head, he saw something scurry across the ice and grab the firestone between its teeth. The light bobbed away followed by a black, lumbering shape. Then, just before he lost consciousness, there was a sudden blinding flash and the ice block shattered into a thousand tiny pieces.

It was the thumping in his brain and the heavy pounding of his heart that pulled Tom from his stupor.

Heaving himself onto one elbow he felt a sharp pain shoot through his arm and something warm trickle down the side of his face. He knew from the familiar stench and the burble of gurgling slime that he was close to the pit. Turning his head, he saw Arcos inhaling the putrid, green smoke, his face contorted to a hideous grin, his grisly band of followers watching.

Tom turned away, a whirl of nausea rising in his throat, and seeing Badger slumped by his feet, he gently stroked the little dog's head. Then he looked around in search of Fergil. But the creature was nowhere in sight. Was that what they were doing, he wondered, witnessing another savage execution?

Suddenly Arcos's voice boomed through the chill, silent air.

'If we had not seen that fool of a boy sneaking through the forest when we were making our way to the Everlasting tree,' he bellowed, 'and had to turn back. We would be there already.'

'But why did you leave the key?' a voice squawked.

'Because I don't need it, you idiot!' Striding arrogantly towards the slavering goblin, Arcos prodded its chest. 'I am the spirit of winter, am I not? I can travel through the portal at any time during the winter period.' When the creature nodded fearfully he grinned, then swaggered back to the centre of the group. 'The wizard however, does need the key. He must change winter to spring before the equinox passes. By leaving the key here, I am preventing him from doing so. And as you all know, if the seasons remain unchanged, Keeros and that dimwit Devole will be completely annihilated.' He grinned wickedly. 'By that time we will all be on earth, watching and waiting for everyone to perish. Without food and warmth, the human race will be unable to sustain life, and when every last one of them is dead . . . their world will be ours. Ha!!'

Tom listed to their chatter, trying desperately to think of what he could do to stop Arcos. Though the firestone was gone he still had his sword, and if the opportunity arose, he was more than ready to use it. After a while, he saw the ice man moving towards him, a trio of lizard headed guards following in his wake.

'Look,' Arcos sneered, dangling a shiny golden chain in front of Tom's face. 'The object for which you came.' As he swung the Charquery key back and forth his eyes glinted menacingly. 'I don't yet know how you and that miserable creature did it.' He pointed at Badger. 'But for destroying my defences, you will both die . . . and your deaths will be excruciatingly painful.'

He leaned down, his fingers reaching for Badger's throat, when Tom leapt to his feet and yanking the sword from its scabbard, lunged straight at him. Beams of dazzling light suddenly shot from the ends of Arcos's long, crystalline fingers. With the force of a bullwhip they snatched the weapon from Tom's hand and sent it careering across the ice. 'Ah yes,' he glowered. 'How well I remember your sword. A very useful weapon!'

While Tom stood there helpless, glaring angrily into the ice man's smouldering eyes, a fat, snub-nosed gremlin snatched the sword from the ground. 'Please master,' it hissed, gazing longingly into the gleaming blade, 'allow me to kill him. Grant me the honour of destroying your enemy.'

A murmur of astonishment rose from the watching crowd. Could the creature be serious? Did it not know of the sword's magic?

'Destroy my enemy?' Arcos scowled, signalling the mob to remain silent.

'Yes master.'

'Is it your greatest desire to please me?'

'Yes master, I want nothing more.'

'And if I allow you this pleasure,' he said, his scowl turning to a hideous, mocking grin, 'what will you give me in return?'

'I give you this master. I picked it from the ground after the explosion.' The gremlin blinked, dazzled by the red light glowing from the firestone. 'It's very pretty master.'

'Pretty!' Arcos shrieked, snatching the crystal from the gremlin's outstretched hand. 'So, this is how . . .'

He stared at the gleaming firestone in disbelief. The only obstacle between himself and universal domination, given to him freely by a half witted imbecile too dim to realise what it had found. The stupid creature deserves to die.

'For this useless piece of glass you want a reward?' he sniggered.

144

'I . . . er . . . no master. I seek no reward . . . I merely wish to serve you master. To destroy your enemy.'

'Then serve me you shall.' Turning to face Tom, his eyes glinted wickedly. 'You will slice off his head!'

'Thank you master. Thank you.'

The crowd snickered and squealed as the gremlin bowed, slung the sword over its shoulder and strode towards Tom. Then a low growl rumbled in its throat as it brought the gleaming blade directly in line with his neck. Turning to Arcos it shouted: 'Let this be proof of my desire to serve you master.'

'Yes. Yes.' Arcos yelled impatiently 'Get on with it!'

'Wait!' Tom cried, glaring scornfully at the iceman. 'He doesn't want you to know that the sword will kill you and not me.'

'Kill me!' The gremlin jerked around so fast it slipped on a patch of ice and when it landed with a hefty thud on its backside, a roar of laughter erupted from the crowd.

'Is it true?' it said, scrambling to its feet. 'The sword will kill me?'

'Don't be so stupid,' Arcos growled. 'The boy lies. He's trying to put you off.'

'Kill, Kill, Kill,' the crowd roared.

'Chop off his head you dumb weasel,' a voice shouted.

'And make it quick' Arcos yelled. 'Or I'll have you thrown into the pit!'

145

'Kill, Kill, Kill,' the crowd chanted again.

The gremlin snatched the sword from the ground and reeling with embarrassment, bounded towards Tom. 'You liar,' it snarled, glaring angrily into his startled eyes. 'You're just trying to save your own skin!' With a sickly grin it swung the weapon back. 'Well you can't!'

There was a loud clang as the blade stopped dead at Tom's neck. Shaking violently, it tore itself from the gremlin's hand, sliced the creature's head clean off then flying through the air slotted itself neatly into the scabbard at Tom's side. But before he had a chance to move, two lizard headed guards grabbed his arms. As Badger ran around their feet snarling viciously, they marched him to Arcos.

'Another exhilarating display,' the ice man sniggered as he reached down and snatched the little dog by the scruff of his neck. 'Let us rid ourselves of these minor irritations.' Marching to the edge of the pit he placed the firestone carefully by his feet then thrust his arm out. 'Watch closely,' he snarled, dangling Badger over the stinking chasm. 'It's your turn next.'

As the crowd fell silent, their bodies rigid with anticipation, their eyes gaping wide, a sinister black shadow darkened the ground. Then a blast of air, so strong it almost knocked them off their feet, whistled past their faces. Looking up they gasped with alarm when they saw the gigantic Gavad Spineclaw swoop over the pit breathing torrents of angry flame.

Flinging Badger to the ground, Arcos swung towards Pendurak. Screaming powerful incantations into the swirling green smoke he inhaled its thickening vapour and as his eyes turned crimson and his face contorted, a loud hum came from deep within the abyss. Thundering to the surface with the speed of a volcanic explosion, a cloud of gargoyle headed demons erupted into the sky, their black, leathery wings sweeping them up like a swarm of hungry bats.

Blasting jet after jet of scorching flame into the whirling throng, Traak swept over them, under and through them, sending hundreds of the creatures fluttering to the ground like scraps of burning paper. But for every one that fell countless more poured from the pit until the sky became a throbbing black mass.

Flocking onto the Spineclaw's back they slid their huge gripping hooks under his steely, impenetrable scales. He dived and twisted, soared and plunged, trying desperately to shake them free. But little by little they crawled onto his head and between the bursts of smoke and flame, crept into his nostrils, singeing and burning in their thousands until the build up of charred bodies extinguished his raging fire.

As Traak tumbled about the sky, his razor sharp talons thrashing and slashing, even more of the batwings gushed from the abyss. Swarming together in one unified mass, they hauled him to the mouth of the stinking pit and with a cohesive screech, tossed him headlong into the gurgling slime. When a cloud of rancid smoke belched into the air they cheered and squealed in triumph, while below them, the demonic creatures witnessing the spectacle, leapt about in a frenzy of exhilaration.

No one but Arcos heard the rumble of galloping hooves thundering across the encampment.

Swinging around, he saw Fergil galloping towards the pit.

'Stop him,' he screamed, his eyes glowing with fury.

147

One of the lizard heads lunged at the galloping steed, but the horse leapt right over its huge, reptilian head and with a forceful kick, sent it crashing to the ground. Landing close to the edge of Pendurak Fergil swung down, snatched the glowing firestone from the earth and was about to hurl it into the pit, when a lightening bolt from Arcos whacked him off his horse.

He hit the ground with a forceful thud, a jolt of searing pain shooting down his spine. His head was throbbing, his body pounding and as a salvo of flashing lights distorted his vision he struggled to he knees. Swinging his arm as far back as he could he flung the pulsating firestone towards the abyss. There was a loud crack as it hit the ground right by the iceman's feet. Grinning cruelly he thrust his hand towards it, but just as his fingers closed around it, Badger leapt across the ice, snatched the crystal from his grasp and with a quick jerk of his head, flung it right into the heart of Pendurak.

A deafening boom thundered across the encampment. The frozen earth started rolling like a storm ravaged sea. Then a gush of crimson smoke shot into the sky and spiralling around the swarm of bat wings, swept them back into the pit.

'No!' Arcos screamed. 'Noooooooo!'

Seizing his chance Tom hurled himself forward and ramming the ice man with all his might, sent him crashing to the ground. Then he quickly snatched the key from around his neck.

'Quick!' he screamed, running to Fergil, 'grab my hand!' But the wound in Fergil's back was bleeding heavily. As he raised his arm a shudder coursed through his body. Then his eyes glazed over and he slumped to the floor.

'You will never leave this place,' Arcos bellowed.

Screaming like a banshee he lunged at Tom and was about to grab the key, when a deafening roar came from deep within the pit. Spinning around, he saw the Spineclaw rising through a cloud of swirling red mist. Clambering onto the land it blasted wave after wave of scorching fire across the encampment, turning half-dead trees to ashes and clusters of ice shelters to sputtering, steaming pools. Then it swung towards the ice man.

But by now Arcos was surrounded by an impenetrable shield of energy that even the Spineclaw's fire could not penetrate. As he screamed frantic incantations at the smouldering pit, his eyes pulsating wildly, his dazzling white robes swirling against a sea of thick, black smoke, Tom hoisted Fergil over his shoulder and with Badger racing ahead, stumbled towards the ice tunnel.

Traak thundered around the enclosure destroying everything in sight, sending hordes of screaming demons stampeding towards the ice palace, when suddenly, a loud, continuous rumble sounded from the distance. As thick, black thunder clouds rolled across the sky and a deluge of jagged hailstones battered the ground, a funnel of twisting wind came speeding towards the encampment. Uprooting trees, flinging huge chunks of ice into the air, it crashed through the perimeter wall. Then it screeched to a sudden halt. Rumbling slowly around it sucked all the black rain clouds from the sky, absorbing them like a sponge until it had doubled in size. Then it suddenly collapsed, hitting the Spineclaw with a deluge of water so powerful, it extinguished his raging fire and sent him spinning across the ground. As he lay on his back struggling like an upturned turtle, too heavy and sodden to flip himself over, a gigantic horned beast clambered from the steaming pit.

149

Thundering across the quagmire it rammed its twisted horns into the leathery flesh above the Spineclaw's eyes, first into one head, then into the other. As he shuddered and groaned it bulldozed his thrashing body to the edge of the abyss and with a hefty thrust, sent him hurtling back into the stinking, gurgling slime.

Arcos emerged from the safety of his protective shield and as the hideous beast roared in triumph, he turned towards the pit. Plunging his arms into the swirling, green smoke, he gave thanks to the dark forces that had kept him from harm. Then he hurried away - his snow-white robes dragging through steaming, muddy pools - towards the dissolving structure of his palace.

He was half way there when the earth started to tremble and an agonising scream ripped the air. Spinning around he saw the enormous horned beast staggering back and forth, its head a gigantic ball of flame. Then as terror flooded his face he watched the Spineclaw rise again from the pit, its thick, leathery scales gleaming like polished steel, its eyes burning with fury.

Heaving his vast body onto the ice, Traak lumbered towards the screaming beast and with one sweep of its powerful tail, sent the howling creature plummeting back into the depths of Pendurak.

Then he turned towards the iceman.

By now Arcos was hurtling across the sodden earth running for his life. He had almost reached the door of the palace - a few strides and he would be there - when a jet of fire suddenly arched through the air, falling in blazing tongues across the entrance. Turning right he headed away. There were other doors around the back. But when he reached the corner another jet of fire shot across his path. Swirling around his trembling body it shot high into the air, encircling him in a searing wall of flame.

As he cowered to the floor, his face white with terror, Traak reached forward and snatching him from the ground, tossed his wriggling body headlong into the smouldering pit.

His screams rang out like shattering glass as he plummeted deep into the depths of Pendurak. Then all of a sudden, a cloud of stinking green smoke burst from the chasm, pumping thousands of ghostly forms into the sky. As they swirled and swayed within the dark vapour, a circle of blinding light appeared at the centre of the cloud, its radiant beams slashing through the fog like piercing blades of steel. When they reached the ghostly spectres howling and writhing at the edge of the mist, the cloud exploded, sending a torrent of black ash cascading to the ground.

As sunlight flooded the encampment the pit of Pendurak gave a final dying gasp then the earth above it rumbled together, until not a single remnant of the evil chasm remained.

Struggling towards the ice tunnel, shielding his eyes from the glare, Tom saw the Spineclaw rise into the sky, swoop low over the blackened remnants of the ice palace, then fly away in the direction of the distant mountains. As his fingers closed around the golden key hanging from his neck, he hitched Fergil further up his back and hoped against hope they would reach the Everlasting tree in time.

CHAPTER 12

The tunnel leading from the encampment was a lattice work of gaping holes, where chunks of melting ice had fallen from the roof. Moving slowly towards it - his face and hands covered with dirty, black smears - Tom scooped Badger from the ground and tucking him under his arm, waded through the pool of icy water blocking his way.

When he reached the two stone Grybb, he slid cautiously between them then turned to his right, intending to retrace his steps along the curve of the ice wall to the spot where he had left the trail. But the ice was melting so fast, the ground beneath the wall had turned into a deep mushy pool that would be impossible to wade through with Fergil on his back. If he was to get the Charquery key to the Everlasting tree in time, he would have to change direction. Turning around, he put Badger down on a narrow but still solid pathway then headed into Bragenon forest.

The silence was creepy enough to make anyone's skin crawl and though shafts of sunlight were now filtering through the treetops, the sickening stench of Pendurak still lingered in the air. Slithering along as fast as he could he dodged mounds of soppy undergrowth and splashed through shallow pools of mushy water. But with Fergil on his back and the ground so slippery, his progress was extremely slow. 'I'll never get there at this rate,' he sighed.

When he finally spotted the trail snaking through the trees a little way ahead, he heaved a sigh of relief. He would at least be able to move faster on flatter ground. But as he headed towards it, a renewed sense of optimism rising in his chest, he heard a strange noise. It sounded like a pole or Skrellk being thumped against the ground. Stopping dead, he yanked Badger behind a tree.

The flaring sunlight made it impossible for him to see properly, but when he peered around the trunk, squinting against the glare, he saw a dark shape jutting from a cluster of trees. Unable to make out what it was he slid around the trunk to view it from the shade. Then he gasped. He couldn't believe it. 'How did you get here?' he yelled, leaping from cover.

Swift was sheltering at the edge of the trail, his eyes bright with shock, his hooves pounding the earth. Seeing Tom, he let out a shrill whiney then trotted anxiously towards him.

'You poor thing,' Tom said, sliding his hand down the horse's neck. 'You must have been scared witless!'

He found a patch of earth that was reasonably dry and set Fergil gently down. The creature's eyes were closed, his skin had turned white, and he didn't appear to be breathing. Fearing the worst, Tom pressed his fingers against Fergil's chest, relieved when he detected the faint flutter of a heartbeat. 'Hang on Fergil,' he whispered, 'Please hang on.'

Moving back to Swift he gently stroked the soft velvety fur around the horse's muzzle. 'You need to do one last thing for me,' he said. 'You must get me back to the Everlasting tree as fast as you can.'

Climbing into the saddle he eased Fergil into the space behind. He wrapped the creature's arms around his waist and slipping his belt around them both, fastened it as tight as he could. Holding the reins in one hand and clutching Fergil's scrawny fingers with the other, he urged Swift into a steady canter.

When they reached the edge of Bragenon Forest they emerged from the trees at the top of the riverbank, close to the spot where the old bridge spanned the glistening water. Tom drew hungrily on the clean, fresh air and as Swift heaved beneath him and Badger flopped to the ground panting, he squinted across the river. The forest looked warm and inviting, the rise and fall of the trees clinging to the land like a gigantic hairy caterpillar. He could see the Everlasting tree standing tall above the rest, but shuddered at the thought of having to cross the river to reach it.

Lifting his head, he carefully examined the sky. It was blue and glistening like a sun drenched sea. But when he turned to his left, he gasped. A dark band of cloud, its edges tinged with yellow, was sliding across the distant mountains towards the forest.

'Hold tight Fergil,' he cried, feeling the creature's head bump lightly against his back as he steered Swift down the grassy slope. 'Whatever happens, don't let go.'

When he reached the bridge he pulled to a halt, his eyes fixing on the gaping hole where he had earlier crashed into the water. Drawing a long, deep breath he tightened his grip on the reins and as a twinge of fear skittered down his spine, he urged Swift forward. 'Steady,' he whispered when the horse's trembling hooves thudded onto the slippery timbers.

They were half way across when the bridge started rattling as though in the grip of a mighty earthquake. With a startled whiney Swift reared up, his eyes flashing with fear, his back legs sliding towards the edge of the planks. 'Steady,' Tom yelled, barely managing to keep the petrified horse from plunging over the side. Then Fergil's hands suddenly slid from his waist. 'No Fergil! Don't let go!'

Steering with one hand, he clamped the other tight around Fergil's scrawny fingers and with his heart thumping wildly, eased Swift back to the centre of the bridge. 'Come on,' he urged, sliding his hand down the jittery animal's neck, 'Nice and steady.' But the terrified creature was so gripped with fear it could move neither forward nor back. At that moment an enormous black shape came slithering through the water towards them. 'Come on Swift. Go!'

The serpent's roaring head burst from the river, its neck arching back in readiness to strike. All of a sudden Swift leapt into the air and screaming in terror, landed with a hefty thud on the bank. 'Go!' Tom roared, the serpent's jaws clashing and crashing as they bolted up the embankment.

Swift galloped along the top of the ridge so fast his hooves barely touched the ground, a whirl of dust rising in his wake.

When safely out of the serpent's reach he pulled to a shuddering stop. Lowering his head, his body heaving in and out, he drew hungrily on the air, while Badger stood by his hooves panting breathlessly.

'We've done it.' Tom yelled, his wide eyes staring back at the river. The agitated serpent was zigzagging through the water jealously guarding its territory. 'Swift, you're incredible!' Turning to Fergil, who by some miracle had managed to remain seated, he heaved a huge sigh of relief.

They moved slowly across the top of the embankment - parallel with the trail running along the edge of the water - until they reached the bush where Tom had hidden from the Skrell. Pulling to a halt he slid the map from his sock. Spreading it as well as he could over the horse's withers, he traced the thin red line running from the river to the centre of the forest. 'We're nearly there,' he whispered.

155

Turning into the trees he joined the trail and sliding the map into his pocket, urged Swift into a steady canter.

***Spears of sunlight sliced across their path as they swept past the bank of giant ferns surrounding the Abalon tree, and soon they were moving through a shady woodland glade, where low hanging branches rustled above their heads and birds twittered noisily in the treetops. As the sweet scent of woodland wafted into his nose, Tom felt as though he had woken from a terrifying dream. But as they drew close to the heart of the forest, Fergil's hands slid from his waist and he felt the creature's spindly body slump against his back. Swinging around he saw that Fergil's eyes had closed and his breathing was jerky and shallow.

'Hang on Fergil,' he said, wrapping the creature's scrawny arms back around his waist. 'Please don't give up. We're nearly there.'

Again he yanked the map from his sock. They only had to pass through a forest clearing then over a rise to reach the Everlasting tree.

He looked up at the sky. The sun was beaming down and there was no sign of the black clouds he had seen moving in from the east.

Stuffing the map into his pocket he urged Swift into a steady walk, he was determined to get Fergil back alive.

When they reached the edge of the clearing he saw the trail snake up a steep incline then disappear into a cluster of trees. Sighing with relief he clasped his hand tight around Fergil's fingers and urged Swift on.

They were half way across the clearing when the birds suddenly stopped twittering and a heavy, oppressive silence descended on the forest. Then, as though a veil was being drawn across the sky, the sunlight gradually faded and a dark, gloomy shadow slid across the ground.

Pulling Swift to a stop, Tom looked up. A band of inky black cloud streaked with flashes of yellow was sliding silently overhead, and through the darkening treetops, he could see the sun sinking slowly towards the horizon.

'No!' he yelled, urging Swift into a gallop. 'I'm sorry Fergil. But we've got to get there fast.'

They flew over the top of the incline and down the other side, where the trail opened out into a wide, straight road. Tom could see the Everlasting tree looming in the distance and as he galloped towards it, several figures ran to meet them, waving their arms and shouting.

'I knew you were the one!' Altair Devole cried, as Swift skidded to a halt. 'I knew it!' But his smile suddenly faded when he saw Fergil slumped against Tom's back. 'Oh dear!' he frowned. 'What happened?'

'Arcos is dead,' Tom panted, 'And the pit has gone - sealed itself up'

He carefully unfastened his belt and sliding from the saddle, eased Fergil gently to the ground.

'Without him,' he gasped, 'Me and Badger would have died. We were about to be thrown into the pit when he brought Traak, the Spineclaw to rescue us. You've got to save him,' he said, looking anxiously into the wizard's eyes.

'He is gravely injured,' Devole said, staring at Fergil with concern. 'The thread of life barely flickers . . . we must hurry.' Turning to Norva he beckoned her to his side. 'Let us hope we're not too late.'

She knelt by Fergil's body and placed her hand on his chest. His heartbeat was weak and his pallor ghostly. Pulling a tiny silver bottle, no bigger than a pearl from her cloak, she quickly squeezed a few drops of colourless liquid onto the creature's withered lips.

She gazed at the spindly little body for several moments, looking for one small movement to show the potion's magic was taking take effect. But Fergil did not stir.

Leaning over him again, she squeezed a few more drops into his mouth, her anxious eyes searching for just one tiny flicker.

'Is he going to be all right?' Tom said weakly.

She placed her hand on Fergil's heart, she could feel nothing - not even the faintest glimmer.

'He can't be dead,' Tom cried. 'Please don't let him die.'

Rising from the ground, her eyes downcast, Norva wrapped her arm gently around Tom's shoulder: 'I'm sorry,' she whispered. 'We're too late.'

No!' Tom screamed. 'He can't die! He just can't.'

Falling to his knees he cradled Fergil in his arms and with tears rolling down his cheeks, Skrellked gently to and fro.

Powerless to ease his pain, Norva stood helplessly by, while Altair Devole shook his head sadly from side to side.

For many long moments no one uttered a sound.

Brushing the tears from his eyes, Tom laid Fergil carefully on the ground and rising to his feet, grabbed hold of the Charquery key. 'You'd better have this,' he sobbed, gazing into the wizard's sorrowful eyes. 'At least he didn't die in vain.'

He was about to lift the chain from around his neck when Norva suddenly grabbed his arm.

'Look!' she cried.'

Swinging around Tom saw Fergil's body shudder.

Rushing to his side he knelt down beside him. As he put his hand gently on Fergil's chest, he felt the creature's heart fluttering beneath his fingers. Then the creature's mouth fell open and he drew a long, heavy breath.

'He's breathing,' Tom yelled.

Fergil's upturned nose began to twitch, his ashen skin suddenly flushed pink and then his huge hooded eyes burst open.

'What's wrong?' he smiled weakly, seeing the astonished looks on their faces. 'Has someone died?'

'Fergil' Tom squealed. 'You're all right!'

'I have to admit,' he said, rising shakily to his feet. 'I have felt better!'

'Thank goodness!' the wizard exclaimed, giving the creature a hefty squeeze. 'Now! I don't wish to appear insensitive, but we must hurry. The sky is yellow, the light is fading fast. Tom, may I have the Charquery Key!'

Grinning like a Cheshire cat, his arm clasped tight around Fergil's shoulder, Tom slid the chain from around his neck and handed the key to the wizard.

'You are brave indeed!' Devole smiled. 'You have completed a monumental task with no concern for yourself. You have passed the test with flying colours and soon you will be honoured.'

'Test! What test? Tom said, frowning.

'All will be revealed, but for now we must make haste. The ceremony must begin before the light gives out completely.'

Smiling, the wizard hurried towards the Everlasting Tree, his eyes dancing with delight as he pushed the key firmly into the golden lock.

'Come together all ye spirits of Keeros,' he smiled. 'Let us herald the spring in peace and harmony.'

Fergil, who was back to normal and chirpier than Tom had ever seen him, was now eager to explore his new surroundings.

'I'm off to take a look around,' he called, trotting away into the forest behind Badger.

'Okay,' Tom said, as he crouched at the edge of the clearing watching Norva and the group of nature spirits form a circle around the Everlasting tree. 'See you later!'

As the wizard stood by, his face beaming like a lantern in the darkness, the group joined hands and circling slowly around the tree began to chant:

'Welcome seasons come and go,
Summer, autumn, winter snow,
Springtime promise here beheld,
All in tune with nature's weld.'

When the wizard lifted a ram's horn to his lips, a thrumming sound - like the swish of a thousand oars slicing though heavy seas - rippled across the sky. Then, as a single, high pitched note rang out - making the darkening clouds tremble like shivering giant - a beam of light shot from the sky, falling directly onto the centre of the golden lock, where the arrow still pointed to winter.

'It is time,' the wizard said.

Leaving the circle Norva moved towards him, her eyes dazzling like two silver orbs.

'Hurry!' he called, handing her a thin, glass rod and a small, silver casket. 'The beam is weak.'

With the tip of the rod she traced a circle in the dusty earth then stepping inside, carefully placed the casket at its centre.

'I call upon the powers of nature to allow me passage through the portal, where I will take my rightful place within the order.'

Turning to the casket she leaned forward to open the lid, when a piercing scream suddenly rang from the woodland.

Spinning around she saw Fergil staggering through the trees, his eyes wide with shock, his blood soaked fingers clutching the shaft of an arrow lodged deep in his chest.

161

As he slumped to his knees gasping for breath, hundreds of archers poured from the forest like ants swarming from a nest.

Quickly surrounding the clearing they formed two concentric circles, one behind the other. The archers at the front dropped to one knee while those behind remained upright, each aiming a deadly arrow at the startled group.

Then a deafening rumble came from the direction of the trail and as everyone turned, they saw a mighty army come thundering towards them.

As the soldiers reached the centre of the clearing they pulled their horses to a halt and thrusting their swords high into the air, sounded a unified roar. Then their leader, a heavily armoured giant of a man, his hairless scalp ringed with heavy, iron studs, his face etched with scars, edged his powerful black stallion forward.

The wizard moved quickly to protect Norva, but as his gaze met the deathly hollows of the warrior's piercing eyes, his hands began to tremble and his face turned ghostly white. 'Grod!' he exclaimed. 'I thought you were . . . '

'It's been a long time Devole! I'm flattered you remember.'

'Remember!' the wizard gasped. 'How could I ever forget?'

The warlord snorted contemptuously then turning his eyes to the cluster of nature spirits huddled beneath the Everlasting Tree, he grinned.

Steering his horse slowly towards them he glared into each of their bewildered faces. Then he swept his gleaming sword across the tops of their heads, smirking as they cowered down in fear.

'Where is Arcos?' he snarled.

'What do you want with Arcos?' the wizard cried.

'What do I want with Arcos?'

The warlord swung his horse about, an evil leer creasing the contours of his heavily jowled face.

'I want what I came for - to pass through the portal to earth. As you well know Devole, only the spirits of winter or spring have access to the portal during equinox. Arcos has agreed to lead us safely through, and by so doing, will ensure his survival when The Shraemen are obliterated. Once Keeros is destroyed, The Dark Warrior Kings will at last be freed from exile and will join us in our conquest of earth. They will bestow us with wealth and power greater than your puny little mind could ever imagine.'

He swung around, his wild eyes blazing.

'Where is Arcos?' he boomed. 'We planned to meet here at the setting of the sun.'

'Your plan has failed!' the wizard cried. 'Arcos is destroyed.'

As he spoke he fumbled with the sleeve of his robe, trying desperately to locate a magic Tarmon twig hidden deep within in the lining. If he could get close enough to touch the warlord with it, he could cast a spell that would send him and his entire army plummeting to oblivion

'You lie, Devole. With the power of Pendurak at his fingertips, Arcos can never be destroyed.'

'See for yourself. We have the key! Arcos is dead!'

As the warlord's eyes darted through the fading light towards the Everlasting tree the wizard lunged forward, a piece of twisted wood gripped tight between his fingers. But as he reached out to cast the spell, a massive broadsword swung across his path almost slicing off his arm. Swerving sideways he caught his foot in the hem of his robe and stumbling awkwardly, sent the Tarmon twig flying across the ground.

At that very moment the light beam flickered.

'Quick!' Devole yelled. 'Turn the key.'

Racing to the lock, her feet thudding across the earth, her heart pounding in her chest, Norva hurled herself forward. But just as she reached out to grab hold of the key, she stumbled.

'We're too late!' the wizard cried as Keeros plunged into darkness.

Struggling to her feet, Norva felt her way around the massive tree trunk. She located the pane of glass covering the front and then fingered her way up until her hand located the key. She swiftly flicked it to the right until it clicked into place. Then she slid to the ground, her eyes searching the darkness for any indication of light.

By now an eerie silence had descended on the forest. Everyone - even the mighty warlord - was standing absolutely still. Listening, waiting, wondering what would happen next.

From somewhere in the distance came a blood curdling howl followed by a heavy thudding noise, like the timbre of heavy footfalls rattling and shaking the ground. Then the grinding creak of trees being ripped from their roots resounded around the forest and from the direction of the mountains came a cacophony of screams and unearthly wails.

The horses immediately took fright, screeching and whinnying, trying to break free from their riders.

Some of the archers were pushing blindly through the darkness trying desperately to find a way out.

Tom was crawling along the ground towards the others, his wrists and elbows scraping painfully on the gritty earth.

'Stay where you are,' the warlord suddenly bellowed. 'Nobody move.'

He urged his horse forward and leaning across its neck, swept his arms backwards and forwards trying to locate the wizard. If the idiot could find the Tarmon twig he thought, maybe he could do something!

But just as he laid his hands on the back of the wizard's neck, a fork of lightening blasted into the clearing. Magnifying the fear on everyone's faces it struck the Everlasting tree.

Suddenly the tree grew exploded into a magnificent, shimmering portal, through which could be seen an endless tunnel of light.

At that very moment, the terrifying sounds of the forest fell silent.

As the darkness slowly lifted everyone gazed into the sky, to the sudden explosion of colour swirling and twirling like a psychedelic work of art. Then, as a radiant yellow sun rose from the horizon, climbing higher and higher until the heavens were saturated with dazzling spears of light, the

165

swirl of colour suddenly blended together and the sky turned to radiant summer blue.

While Grod stood transfixed, his attention captured not by the sky but by the magnificent shimmering portal, the wizard snatched the Tarmon twig from the ground. Swinging towards the warlord, he reached out to cast a spell, but just as he thrust forward, an arrow thudded deep into his back. As the colour drained from his face he let out a loud, shuddering gasp and crashed to the ground.

'Out of my way!' the warlord growled, bulldozing through the crowd circling around the wizard's body.

'You!' He grabbed Norva by the hair, dragging her viciously towards the portal. 'You will lead us through.'

'No!' Tom yelled, trying to bar the warlord's way. But two mounted warriors swiftly grabbed him by the arms and hoisting him from the ground, dangled his wriggling body between them. 'Norva, don't do it!' he pleaded.

The warlord snarled, his dark eyes squeezed to slits, then he nodded to the horsemen who slowly pulled apart until Tom was screaming in agony.

Sliding a small, silver dagger from her cloak, Norva jabbed it into the back of the warlord's hand.

'Arghh!' he yelled, letting go of her hair as he swung sharply round.

'Kill him, and you kill me,' she cried, holding the thin, razor sharp blade against her throat. 'If I die, you will never get through the portal.'

'You wouldn't dare,' the warlord breathed.

166

Pressing the dagger until a dimple formed in the soft skin on her neck, Norva glared defiantly into his furious black eyes. 'I would do anything to stop you.'

There was a moment of tense silence when neither of them moved. Then she pressed down harder, until a thin line of blood trickled down her neck.

'Release him!' Grod shouted, signalling to the horsemen.

As Tom crashed to the ground Norva rushed to his side. But within seconds, dozens of arrows were aiming at the huddle of nature spirits clustered around the wizard's body.

'Now!' the warlord bellowed as one of the horsemen leaned down and quickly snatched the dagger from Norva's fingers. 'Lead us through the portal, or they all die.'

'No!' someone shouted. 'Don't do it . . . we would rather die than . . .'

'Do as I say or each and every one of them will be flayed alive, while you . . . ' he jabbed his finger at Norva, '. . . will have the pleasure of witnessing their suffering.

To Norva the thought was unbearable.

'I will take you through,' she whispered, her voice weak and quivering. 'But before we can cross from one dimension to the other, I must complete the ritual.' She rose weakly to her feet and with faltering steps moved to the spot where she had earlier traced a circle on the ground.

'Be warned!' the warlord growled. 'Any tricks, and they all die.'

Standing by the silver casket, her eyes filled with tears, she again called upon the forces of nature to grant her safe passage through the portal. As her trembling fingers lifted the lid a vibrant white light arched from the casket, forming a magnificent translucent bridge across the gap between herself and the Everlasting Tree.

'It is done,' she whispered tearfully.

As the warlord roared in triumph, Tom crouched at the edge of the clearing clutching Badger to his chest. He couldn't believe that they had gone this far, stared victory in the face only to have it so cruelly snatched away. His body was shivering as he gazed along the columns of Grod's soldiers stretching down the Trail of Medioc - an army of death ready to invade his world.

His eyes slid across the contrasting beauty of the woodland, where birds twittered high in the shimmering treetops and the glow of dappled sunlight bathed the forest floor.

As a wave of nausea swept over him, he cradled his head in his hands. Then he noticed something glinting in the corner of his vision.

Jerking around he saw the soldiers sheathing their swords in readiness to move - but the glimmer had not come from them - it had come from a dense patch of woodland close to the edge of the trail.

As Grod's powerful voice boomed a command the archers stood to attention and forming a neat line, marched silently to the rear of the cavalry.

When the army was finally in place, the warlord rode across the clearing towards the Everlasting tree, where Norva was slumped by the portal, her dull eyes staring at the ground, her face filled with sadness. As he reached the translucent bridge he swung around to face his troops.

'Let victory begin,' he roared, thrusting his sword high above his head.

At that moment a gigantic warrior burst from the forest, his scarlet cloak billowing like a burning sail, his armour glinting like a sun drenched sea. As his wild-eyed stallion reared and whinnied thousands of soldiers poured from the woodland, descending on Grod's army like a plague of hungry locusts.

The clash of hostile steel rang out, a hail of arrows whipped the air, horses screamed, warriors fell, blood flowed free from mortal wounds.

Above the pandemonium came a thunderous, spine-chilling roar as Valtok's searching eyes locked on the object of his hatred. With fury twisting his war-ravaged face and anger almost bursting his heart, he charged at the startled warlord like a frenzied bull.

Thrusting up his shield Grod caught the strike full on, but its force was so fierce, so driven by fury it almost whacked him off his horse. Quickly recovering his composure, he spun around and sounding an angry war cry, he lunged at the raging warrior.

Valtok fought like a man possessed, raining blow after furious blow on his detested enemy. With every strike his wild eyes flashed, at each clash of steel his voice roared loud. He swiped and slashed, thrust and parried, charged at the warlord again and again until finally, when dazed and weakened, the evil tyrant began to sway unsteadily in his saddle. Then came the crushing blow that sent him plummeting to the ground.

169

Leaping from his horse, roaring like a half-crazed lion, Valtok swept in for the kill, but before he had chance to strike, one of Grod's injured soldiers suddenly hurled himself across the warrior's path, sending his massive body crashing to the ground.

Screaming with victory, Grod leapt to his feet and diving forward, plunged his sword deep into Valtok's chest. The warrior's massive hands grabbed hold of the blade, blood oozing through his fingers as he struggled to wrench it free, but as he glared into the warlord's merciless eyes, the evil monster thrust the weapon down, right through his heart.

Remounting his powerful, black stallion Grod turned to the blood soaked battlefield strewn with the war-ravaged bodies of his soldiers. His army had been swiftly annihilated and now the victors stood before him in shocked silence - their conquest swift, their triumph complete.

But without their leader they were nothing.

He thrust his blood spattered sword into the air, his dark, malignant eyes sweeping their stunned faces. Not one of them had the power to kill him. Only a true Zengal Knight could do that, and the last Zengal Knight was dead.

Turning to Norva, who was standing with the other nature spirits clustered around the wizard's body, her ashen face blank with shock, her eyes awash with tears, he grinned. Now she would take him through the portal. And no one would stop him - no one could stop him. He was invincible.

But as he steered his horse towards her something caught his eye, something obscured by the ragged lines of soldiers blocking the trail.

Curious, he pulled to a halt, and rising in his stirrups, narrowed his eyes to slits. Peering into the shadow of the forest he saw a carriage jutting from the edge of the trees. Puzzled, he stared at the pair of matching horses, their gleaming black harnesses glistening against the blinding whiteness of their coats.

'Arcos!' he suddenly bellowed, urging his horse forward, 'I knew that fool Devole was lying!'

He threaded his way through the silent lines of Valtok's soldiers, who, offering no resistance stood aside to let him pass. Pathetic cowards he thought as he felt their resentful eyes boring into him, hating him, wishing he were dead.

When he neared the end of the trail he halted. About twenty soldiers were standing across the path blocking his way. Let's see how brave they really are. When he sliced his sword through the air they gradually pulled apart. Cowards the lot of them, he sniggered.

As he passed slowly between them his dark, brooding eyes drilled into each and every one of their solemn faces - they were no match for him and they knew it.

When he reached the end of the line he swung his head in the direction of the carriage and what he saw made him gasp in horror.

Standing in the dappled half-light was the hunched, twisted remnant of a man. His mutilated face bore no resemblance to the strong, handsome face it once was. Distorted lips barely covered the toothless mouth. Crushed, sunken cheekbones met a distended lower jaw and wispy tufts of silver white hair hung from the heavily disfigured scalp. The ears were missing, the nose was missing, but the piercing, tortured, vengeance seeking eyes were in tact. The eyes of

171

Drogon - last of the mighty Zengal Knights - the withered sticks of his gnarled fingers curled around the trigger of a crossbow.

'Drogon!' the warlord breathed, suddenly swinging his horse about. He must get out of the way before the idiot could take aim. But hundreds of Valtok's soldiers were blocking his way and more were flooding from the woods, thwarting an escape through the trees.

His only choice was to fight - this pathetic creature was no match for him.

If he could dodge the bolt from the crossbow he would slice off Drogon's head before he even had a chance to reload.

Swinging around he swept up his sword, thrust up his shield until it was level with the bridge of his nose, then digging his spurs hard into the stallion's flanks he set off at full gallop.

As he thundered along the trail something whistled past his head missing him by inches. 'Idiot!' he grinned. 'You've just signed your own death warrant.'

But as the warlord raced towards his target, swinging his sword in readiness to strike, he heard a loud click then another shrill whistle and before he knew what was happening, a crossbow bolt hit him right between the eyes.

His vision suddenly blurred, his head started booming like a cannon and feeling his body swaying he grabbed hold of the stallion's mane to stop himself from falling. But when the horse drew close to Drogon it suddenly swerved around, flinging the evil warlord to the ground.

As he lay there dazed and bleeding, the sword still clamped in his fist, he blinked to clear the dark haze floating in front of his eyes. Then he let out a violent roar. Fighting the whir of dizziness pounding in his brain, he struggled to his feet. He could see a hazy shape standing before him. Swaying from side to side he lifted his sword with both hands, his arms quivering under its weight as he staggered forward.

But just as he swung the weapon back, a cloud of darkness enveloped him. Then his knees suddenly buckled, his eyes glazed over and his massive body crashed to the ground.

The evil tyrant, at last, was dead.

Pulling the hood of his robe far enough over his head to cover his face, Drogon lifted the warlord's sword from the ground. He gazed into the blood spattered blade for a long time, his head bowed low and his body shaking.

Then, handing it to one of his soldiers he stared down the trail. Tom and Badger were racing towards him, darting in and out of the mass of cheering warriors.

'Thank goodness you came,' the boy cried as he skidded to a halt. 'It's been awful. There are many dead. Fergil tried to warn us but they shot him in the back, the wizard too, and Valtok . . . Valtok is . . . '

'I know,' Drogon whispered, laying his crumpled fingers gently on Tom's shoulder. 'Come, take me to him.'

Leaning on Tom for support, he hobbled slowly along the trail until they reached the place where Valtok's body lay.

'My brother was a noble Knight of Zengal,' Drogon said. 'Sworn to lay down his life for the protection of these lands.' Lowering himself painfully to the ground he placed his withered fingers gently on the warrior's sword arm. 'I came too late,' he whispered. And in the pained, empty stillness, he silently wept.

It was not long afterwards that Drogon and the Zengal army escorted their burdens of grief away. The bodies of Valtok and Fergil lay side by side on the carriage roof and as Tom watched it shrink slowly into the distance, he tried hard to choke back his tears.

He was staring down the empty trail long after the cortège had gone, trying desperately to come to terms with what remained of his nightmare. Altair Devole was dead, Arcos the spirit of winter had been thrown into the pit. Without them the delicate balance of nature would be destroyed. How could life on earth continue now?

In his confusion he looked around. Norva was standing with the others by the wizard's body. He should go to her, ask her what to do, but overcome with despair he lifted Badger into his arms and instead headed towards the Everlasting Tree.

Staring into the shimmering portal he suddenly felt an overwhelming desire to enter the void, to travel the unknown road - a road back to his own world.

Shielding his eyes against the glare he stepped nervously onto the translucent bridge. It was light and airy, filled with the colours of the rainbow and as he edged forward, he felt like he was floating on air.

When half way across he stopped. He could see an old man standing in the tunnel of light, his body frail and bent, his weathered face showing the painful burden of age. Tom recognised the figure. It was himself - the way he was on earth - the way he would be again should he return.

He looked down at the soft, warm body nestled in his arms - on earth Badger no longer existed. Lowering his head, he buried his face in the little dog's fur. He felt bewildered, divided, trapped between the parameters of two worlds, and in his confusion he wept.

'This is no time for sadness!' a familiar voice shouted from behind. 'We won!'

Tom stiffened, his head shot up, and certain his ears were deceiving him, he darted around. The wizard was standing at the end of the bridge, a broad smile lighting up his face and his mischievous eyes twinkling like stars.

'But you're . . . you were killed!' Tom shrieked. 'Over there! I saw you. You're dead!'

'Not dead,' the wizard chuckled. 'I was er . . . regenerating . . . it takes time you know!'

As he walked off the bridge and put Badger on the ground, Tom's eyes never left the wizard's face.

'Because of you our worlds are safe. Keeros will be glorious again and the seasons of earth will continue much as before.'

'But . . . that's impossible,' Tom said. 'Arcos is gone. The Spineclaw threw him into the pit.'

'On Keeros, nothing is impossible,' the wizard smiled. 'Later I will explain, but for now we must get Norva quickly on her way. The winter perils of your world need urgent attention.'

He beckoned the group of nature spirits who, one by one stepped onto the shimmering bridge and as they reached the centre they vanished into thin air.

Norva was the last to cross but before she stepped onto the bridge she placed her hand gently on Tom's shoulder.

'We have much to thank you for,' she said. She leaned forward and gently kissed him on the cheek - which made him blush and feel extremely embarrassed. Then she moved across the bridge towards the shimmering portal, and as she entered the prism of light, she drifted effortlessly away.

'At last!' the wizard said, as the bridge disintegrated and the Everlasting tree returned to its former glory. 'It is done. Come,' he smiled, 'we will return to the Abalon tree. There is much to discuss and decisions to be made.'

When they arrived at the Abalon tree they pushed through the sunny garden then navigated the dark, spiral stairway with the help of an illuminated glass rod.

Tom felt an inexplicable quiver of excitement as the wizard pushed open the little wooden door at the bottom of the stairs. As his eyes slid across the jumble of old books lining the bulging shelves and the mass of strange objects cluttering the floor, a deep sense of belonging wafted over him.

'The trials you have endured were a test,' the wizard said as they entered the room. 'We had to be certain you were the rightful one.'

'The rightful one?' Tom said, frowning. What do you mean?'

'You are the only mortal who could succeed in returning the Charquery key, and for reasons I will explain later, it was vital that we find you. But we had to be sure of your ability to overcome evil and prove yourself worthy of a place within Shraemen hierarchy.'

'What?' Tom looked completely baffled.

'To protect you we sent a Sylph - an air spirit. He was to keep watch over you, monitor your journey and return regularly with news of your progress. He was forbidden to intervene unless your life was in mortal danger.'

The wizard turned to the portrait of an enormous bird hanging on the wall at the other side of the room.

'Sylphs can take any form they choose,' he said. 'A bird, a dragonfly, a moth, or even a gust of wind. They belong to the air and are within everything that is natural and good, both in your world and in ours. This bird is the Skrell - creature of mystery and legend.'

'But I don't understand.' Tom exclaimed, staring at the portrait. 'The bird I saw was also a man . . . Lyal!'

'This beautiful creature is just one of Lyal's many guises. He chose it to help protect you from the serpent Pyrus Thangor. Skrells and water serpents have been at odds with each other since the dawn of time. Lyal took this form in the hope that it would distract Thangor's attention away from you.'

The wizard moved towards a large globe floating in mid air in a corner of the room. Tom could see it was a replica of earth by the meticulously detailed countries and oceans illustrated on its surface. The wizard spun it round until the images became a blur and tapping his chin thoughtfully, stared directly into Tom's eyes.

'Do you like it here?' he asked.

'Without all the bad stuff, it's great!' Tom smiled.

'Good! I was hoping you would say that.' He spun the globe again. 'If you were given the choice to stay here forever or return to earth as you are now, with provision made for your requirements of course, what would you choose?'

Tom's mouth fell open. 'I . . . I don't know,' he said, 'I like it here, but . . .'

He turned to the comfy old armchair where Badger had curled into a ball and was sleeping soundly. Reaching down he stroked the little dog's head and as Badger opened his sleepy eyes, he gave a half hearted wag of his tale then gently licked the boy's hand.

'If I return to earth,' Tom said. 'Can Badger go with me? I couldn't bear to leave him again.'

'Unfortunately not,' the wizard said, shaking his head sadly. 'On earth he no longer exists.'

'That's what I thought,' Tom sighed.

Smiling gently, the wizard moved to the other side of the room, where a huge wooden carving representing the four seasons covered a large portion of the wall. He pointed to the section depicting winter.

'Without Arcos, the seasons are incomplete - the delicate balance deficient. To ensure continuation of the cycle, the spirit of winter must be replaced. As I am the only one who possesses enough knowledge, it is I who must fulfil the task. That will leave us with a problem. We must find someone to take my place. Someone capable of keeping the fragile balance in tact.'

.'But who could that be?' Tom gasped, as the wizard made his way back towards him. 'I mean . . . who could replace the Eastern wizard?'

'If you agree,' Devole smiled, 'It will be you. You will remain here as my pupil.'

'Your pupil?' Tom squeaked.

'You will embrace all of my knowledge, assume the complex secrets of the universe, and when the time comes and you are sufficiently prepared, you will take my place as the Eastern wizard, maintaining nature's delicate balance, ensuring all things are kept in perfect harmony. Only the rightful one can do so.'

'But , , ,' Tom felt as though he had just been hit by a ten-ton hammer. 'There isn't time! To learn to be a wizard I mean . . . It will take ages!'

'It is true there is much to be done, and you are right, it will take a long time. But remember, a day on Keeros is equal to a week on earth and with winter just ending, there is plenty of time before I need to take on my new responsibilities. You will be amazed at how quickly you will learn and if I arrange to make next winter very mild indeed, it will give me more time to devote to your education.'

'Yes!' Tom cried, his voice positively quivering with exhilaration. 'Of course I will stay!'

At that moment Badger leapt from the comfy old armchair and raced around the room squealing with excitement. It was as if he had understood every word that had been said.

As the wizard raised his eyebrows his spectacles slide to the end of his nose, making Tom laugh so loud he almost toppled over.

There, in that cosy, cluttered room somewhere on the edge of time, the dawn of a new age was about to begin.

CHAPTER 14

As the sun burst from the clouds and a warm breeze swept down the hillsides, the ancient village of Tambley Croft burst into life. Cottage doors flew open, people crowded into the narrow lanes and walkways, jabbering and squawking as though some amazing phenomenon had occurred.

Shielding their eyes against the glare they gazed into the sky, and as if they had never in all their lives seen such a magnificent sight, their mouths fell open and they gasped.

Children ran about giggling and squealing and rolling over and over in the rapidly melting ice until their clothes were soaking wet. But nobody cared - they were all too filled with relief to worry.

Betty Briggs and Maggie Bradshaw were tramping towards Brantham Tor, just ahead of Fergus Benson and Bob Trimble, when the magical transformation occurred.

'Look!' Maggie cried, squinting across the sun drenched valley, 'it's starting to thaw!'

'It's about time,' Betty grumbled, 'considerin' how long we've been frozen up.' Loosening the shawl from around her head, she pointed towards the Tor. 'It's not far now lads,' she called. 'He's up on Molly's Crag, just beyond those trees.'

'I wish we hadn't.' Maggie said, staring towards the Skrellky incline. 'He's not done anything wrong.'

'Hush!' Betty scolded. 'We're bringing the lads here with good reason. All that grass 'n flowers in the middle of the worst freeze we've ever known! There's something fishy going on and I aim to find out what it is. Over there lads! Look!'

She pointed to the top of the crag, where a dark shape was hunched at the centre of a circle of daffodils.

'See what I mean!' she declared. 'Flowers in the middle of winter!'.

'Get the rope ready,' Fergus whispered, swinging a shotgun from his shoulder.

'Rope!' Maggie exclaimed angrily. 'He's an old man you fool. You don't need rope. And you certainly don't need a shotgun!'

'Don't you be so sure missus! We've 'ad some strange characters round 'ere this past year. An' if you knew wot I know,' he winked at her knowingly, 'You wouldn't sleep sound in yer bed at night.'

'Rubbish!' Maggie shouted. 'You're just trying to scare us into thinking your something special. That's all!'

Stamping her frozen feet, she barged ahead irritably.

'I wouldn't get too close missus.' Fergus called after her.

But it was no use. Maggie was determined to get to Tom Goodwin before anyone else.

'You'll not stop her once her minds made up,' Betty chuckled. 'She's a stubborn one is that. Anyway, if he so much as moves . . . shoot 'im!'

When Maggie reached the top of the slope she stared wide eyed at the shabby, old overcoat bunched up at the centre of the grass circle.

'Thank goodness,' she whispered, looking all around as she stepped carefully over the daffodils. 'He's gone.'

Lifting the damp coat from the ground she fished into one of the pockets. It felt empty at first - then her fingers touched something small and round, wedged into one of the corners. 'What's this?' she muttered, grabbing the tiny object between her finger and thumb and yanking it out. It was a shiny farthing. Turning it over she carefully examined the date - 1896.

Suddenly her heart skipped a beat and her mind raced back to the day Tom ran away to sea. She would never forget it. And to make sure he wouldn't forget her, she gave him a brand new shiny farthing. 'You know what?' he had said, when her eyes filled with tears. 'One day I'm going to do something special - something amazing. And when I do. I'll get this back to you, just so as you'll know.'

'I knew it was you,' she whispered, as a tear trickled slowly down her face. 'And I knew one day you would bring it back.'

'Well, I'll be!' shouted Fergus, staring at the grass and flowers as he popped his head over the incline. 'I ain't seen nowt like this before. Not in the middle of a freeze!'

'He's gone!' Maggie barked, sniffing away the tears as she slipped the coin into her pocket. 'He left his coat! Look!' She held the garment up.

'Gone?' shouted Betty, struggling to clamber over the top of the rise, 'Do you mean he's d . . . ?'

'He's not here,' Maggie bellowed. 'He's disappeared.'

183

Betty strode determinedly across the grass and grabbing the coat, plunged her hand into one of the pockets. 'Let's have a look!' she said, pulling out a crumpled piece of paper. 'Oh dear . . . Oh lord . . . I *was* right! It says Thomas Goodwin, Canning Street Library. There's a date as well, but the ink's all smudged and I can't make it out. Well I never!' she exclaimed, swinging around and glaring at Maggie. 'And you wouldn't believe me!'

'Who the 'eck's Tom Goodwin?' Bob and Fergus chorused in unison.

'He was a strange 'un.' Betty said, her voice lowering in pitch as her eyes darted from one to the other. 'Always on his own. After his dog drownded in the river he went a bit weird. Blamed 'imself yer see. Anyway, one day he locked his step-dad up, threw away all his food and took off. Vanished! Was never, ever seen again. Some said he was found in the river, drownded just like his dog. Others said he'd been carted off to a looney bin. I don't know what happened to him, neither does Maggie. But I can't imagine why he came back.'

'What I can't fathom,' said Fergus, scratching his head, 'is why there's footprints leadin' up 'ere, deep ones like as if they've been melted into the ice, but there's none goin' back down. Looks like as if 'e just vanished into thin air. Very strange! Anyway, we'll 'ave a quick look around then we'd best get back to the village.'

'Well!' Betty cried, following Maggie carefully down the slope. 'There's one thing for sure. Tom Goodwin won't be missed. He never did any good for anyone!'

'That's what you think!' Maggie murmured, squeezing the little shiny farthing tight between her fingers.

The end

19809652R00106

Printed in Great Britain
by Amazon